—— From a ——
WATERFALL

JILL ARLAND

PAGE PUBLISHING, INC.
Conneaut Lake, PA

First originally published by Page Publishing 2020

ISBN 978-1-6624-2992-7 (pbk)
ISBN 978-1-6624-2993-4 (digital)

Printed in the United States of America

Contents

The sound of my bare feet slapping against the nighttime cold street is what really started it for me. I never knew life could feel like that. I didn't know my smile could stretch so real. It's true that I wasn't really feeling anything. Not in the sense that my friends asked me if I was anyway, but I felt real. I felt happy. I felt alive. I felt old. I was in seventh grade. That was when I climbed out of the covering that all children are born with. I pulled it off and climbed out one foot at a time, weary at first, and then vibrant. I still can't quite put into words what my smile looked like besides saying that I was defenseless against it.

Part 1

APRIL 1998

Chapter 1

WHO WE ARE

Thomas, Nicole, and I have been existing together forever. We live across the street from each other, and our parents met each other when we still lived within them. I don't remember life without the two of them. Nicole and I are in ninth grade; Thomas and our other best friend Lily are in tenth. The four of us spend every second that we can together. At fourteen, there is plenty about life that I really don't understand yet, but I do know that our friendship is special. We need each other not only to exist, but to maneuver this scary world that is full of unknowns.

We are all sitting in Thomas's room. Hole's "Celebrity Skin" blares from the radio. The music distributes itself within the cacophony of our own four voices talking, laughing, and filling the room. Thomas starts laughing as his sister slides off of his elevated bed and accidentally falls on the floor. We all giggle at Nicole's mishap, but Thomas can't seem to stop. He laughs and laughs until he begins to make odd gasping noises. His laughing makes the rest of us start again. We just keep going—no one can stop now. Thomas's mom walks in the room.

"Jess, ya motha just called. She wants ya home for dinna." She briefly takes in her surroundings. "What the hell are ya, idiots, laughing at?"

This makes it even worse. We start all over again. We are all laughing, rolling, dying. I manage to pull myself together enough to walk out of his room and onto the adjoining deck, where I tell my friends that I will be back as soon as I'm done eating.

As soon as I walk in the door, I sit at the table. I want to finish eating as soon as I can so I can go back across the street. I am the only one who has to sit down every night for a family dinner. I just want to be with my friends.

"Jess, what the hell are ya wearing? That guy is a freakin' weirdo."

That's my brother Matt. I don't say anything. I just smile and look at my mother. She makes me go to my room and take off my Marilyn Manson T-shirt. It makes me so happy that she can't throw away the shirt because it isn't mine. My own way of getting back at her after throwing out *Portrait of an American Family*. After dinner, I am only allowed to go back across the street for another half an hour before I have to be back home. It is Friday, but my mother forces me to be home at 9:00 PM, no matter what day it is.

After a typical dinner filled with inquiries about my day from my mother and rude side comments about my music preferences from my brother, I go back across the street. I walk directly through the back gate, up the deck stairs, and into Thomas's room where he and Lily are sharing a cigarette. She is sitting on his bed while he sits on the computer. "Jumper" hums in the background.

Thomas and Lily used to date. He met Lily in eighth grade, and they soon started going out. When Thomas finally came out, Lily was distraught for a long while. The pain of what went on during that time sometimes still emerges from Lily, especially when we are drinking. He was her first love and still is her best friend. This may have killed other girls and left them with a wound too large to fix, but not Lily.

Tomorrow we are planning on getting drunk in the middle of the day, one of our favorite things to do. My mom will be working. She is a nurse and works every other weekend. Matt will be home with me. My brother Matt is three years older than me. He is a senior in our high school. He doesn't talk to anyone. He pretty much keeps to himself. The extent of his socialization is when either me or one of my friends goes and sits with him at lunch.

"Hey, Lily, are you sleepin' over here?" I ask as soon as I walk into the room.

"Yea, I think so. I just have to call my dad and let him know."

"How are we going to get forties tomorrow? Can your mom get them for us?" I ask Thomas, hopeful for a positive answer.

"My mom is being mean. I asked her before when you left, and she said no."

"Oh, that sucks," I say, and then reply, "Then I guess we will have to wait outside of 7-Eleven. Can I have a cigarette before I have to go home?"

Lily takes one Marlboro Light from her lunchbox and lights it. I happily jump up next to her on Thomas's bed. The first drag after dinner is always the best.

"Hey, where's your sister?" I ask Thomas.

"My mother bribed her to go to 7-Eleven and get cigarettes for her."

"You let her go by herself?"

"I didn't feel like going."

"Oh, that's mean. Hey, Lil, you wanna go meet her halfway. I kinda wanna go for a walk?" Lily briefly looks from me to Thomas.

"Okay, Thomas we'll be back in a few minutes," Lily says.

Thomas immediately attaches himself to Lily's arm and pulls her near him, "Noooooooooooo, don't leave me."

She just smiles and says, "We'll be right back."

"Come on, guys, pleeeeease don't go," Thomas whines.

"We'll be back in like five minutes," I say quickly and grab Lily out of Thomas's grasp before he can talk her into staying.

Lily and I walk out of the sliding door that is connected to Thomas's room directly into the biting April evening. Lily takes another drag and hands me the cigarette. I take two calming drags before handing it back to her. Just as I hand her back the cigarette, an obnoxiously loud car speeds past us. Someone screams randomness out of the car window. This scares me so much that I jump onto Lily, mashing my cheek against her shoulder and locking my elbow with hers. She laughs her quiet laugh, and we speed up. At the corner, we see Nicole smoking one of her mother's cigarettes and talking to a group of boys. She isn't scared of anything. Once we catch up, we realize that the boys are complete strangers. As soon as we approach, the boys walk away.

Now that we have Nicole back, the three of us link our arms together and walk to our "smoking spot"—a row of overgrown pine trees that continue to provide us with shade, shelter, and serenity.

"Hey, do you, guys, want to sneak out tonight?" Nicole asks.

"And do what?" Lily responds absently.

"I told Pat that we would meet him at the high school on the steps at one. We should get forties."

"Well, let's go back to your house and ask Thomas. Do you want to, Jess?"

"I will only go if we all go," I say.

Both Lily and Nicole also say that they will go. Even though I know that Thomas will agree to go if the rest of us do. I say, "Okay, well you, guys, can ask your brother when you get back to your house, but we need to hurry up because I need to go home."

"Chill out, Jess, let me finish my cigarette," Nicole raspingly reacts.

Nicole's harshness may seem unwarranted to some, but Lily and I know that that is just how she is.

"Fe-fi-fo-fum! I smell...the fingerprints of scum!" I suddenly shout, quoting *Ace Ventura: When Nature Calls*.

I say it over and over until finally Nicole and Lily yell for me to stop. I, of course, think them telling me to stop is hysterical. I laugh my really throaty, soul shining kind of laugh. I then roll out of my Indian-style and kick my legs up in the air. I have one leg straight up pointing toward the stars, and the other one bent in a Peter Pan-esque pose. Still laughing, Nicole leans over and slaps my ass really, really hard.

"Ow, you, bitch!" I instantly yell out in my throaty grumble.

I am not being mean; this is one of our phrases that we frequently use. Thomas yelled this at his sister a few years ago when she hit him, and it was so funny to hear Thomas curse—an obvious indicator that he doesn't do it often—that we all just lost it when he was trying to be serious. Now I am rolling around on the floor, saying it over and over and we all laugh.

We walk toward our houses, and I depart at the corner and say goodnight to Lily and Nicole. I am sad to leave these people who make me feel whole, but I am happy. I have that tickling scary kind of excitement doing the backstroke through my veins. After waving my shirt through the night to remove the smell of badness, I return home. I listen to K-Rock on the radio as I doze off and wait for the knocking on my window to call me back to comfort.

Chapter 2

SNEAKING OUT

The knocking wakes me up instantly. I am so attuned to it. I hang my head out of the window so that they know I'm awake. I signal, indicating that I will be right there. I slip on my hoodie, open my window, then the screen, and climb out of the window, balancing on the railing that leads to the front steps of our house. Once I am safely on the ground, without saying anything we head toward 7-Eleven. Once we are a safe distance from our houses, I finally begin to breathe. This is Thomas's cue to turn on his little handheld radio. Fuel's "Shimmer" blares out, a cue that our night has commenced. Once we get to 7-Eleven, we argue over who is going to ask the first two people to buy us beer. Nicole is the winner; she doesn't have the same sense of embarrassment as the rest of us. I swear she is wired without it.

"Excuse me sir, do you think you can do me a favor?" Nicole asks the first person who pulls in.

This man doesn't even acknowledge her. He just walks right in without even looking at her. He is a young guy, probably in his early twenties. We all swear that when we are his age, we will do favors for kids like us. We all sit on the cement, passing around one of Thomas and Nicole's mom's Marlboro Light 100's. Another car pulls in with music blasting. Perfect. Music blasting is always a good sign. Nicole gets up and practically runs over to her prey. Sometimes these guys are quick.

"Excuse me, sir, do you think you can do me a favor?"

"Lemme guess, buy you cigarettes or beer?"

"Can you get us four forties of Olde E?" Nicole asks.

The man looks around quickly. "Yea, okay, gimmie ya money."

Nicole hands the man a small stack of dollar bills and a handful of quarters.

"You've gotta be kiddin' me with these quarters," the man replies.

Nicole just smiles and thanks her prince. She runs back over to the rest of us where we whisper excitedly. We know we are very lucky. That was mighty quick.

When the man walks out, he looks around one more time and chucks the beer into our open arms. We thank him wholeheartedly and continue on our way. We walk at a quick pace and head to the high school. The gigantic giraffe-like lampposts that light up the highway are strangely alluring. They comfort me.

"Oh crap!" I hear Thomas say from up ahead.

"What?" we all say at about a second apart.

"The batteries on my radio died. Now we have no music."

After replying with short bursts of different variations of "that sucks," we forget about it. We walk for a few more minutes before there is a rare few moments of silence. I promptly break it by bursting out with one of our usual Beatles classics. Everyone joins in with their predetermined parts, which are easily accessible from years of practice. We continue to walk and sing and talk and eventually we arrive at the high school. We automatically climb the dozen or so steps to our throne. We immediately open our prizes and begin our passage. We talk about everything and nothing. Obnoxious laughter escapes, the passing of ChapStick, chugging competitions, breakouts into song, and peeing behind bushes makes up a majority of our time.

"Hey, does anyone know what time it is?" I ask.

Thomas looks at his watch. "Two eleven…ahhhhhhhhhhhh-hhh…It happened again. Why does this keep happening? Lily…I'm scared."

Thomas jumps onto Lily's lap, and the rest of us jump close and hang onto each other. We call it the "Eleven Disease." Every time we look at a clock, it is something eleven. We feel it must be a sign. We are all irrationally afraid of elevens.

"Just stop thinking about it, guys."

"Thomas, you're making it worse. Let's talk about something else," Lily says.

I know that she is really scared too, but I belt out, "I've got fidgety feet, fidgety feet, fidgety feet! / Oh, what fidgety feet, fidgety feet, fidgety feet! / Say, mate, come and be my sway-mate…"

I think this makes everyone feel better. It makes me feel better. I am feeling unrestrained, lovely.

"Hey, Nicole, what time is Pat supposed to be here?" I ask.

"Oh, he was supposed to be here at one. I wonder if he's still coming."

"Oh, I bet he couldn't wake up again."

I really like Pat, but I am covertly pleased to have my best friends to myself.

"Hey, let's push that huge flowerpot down the steps," Thomas says as he looks over at this massive barrel of a flowerpot that is empty of flowers but filled with dirt. Personally I am scared to do it. I am scared to do anything for fear of my mother's wrath. Lily and I agree that we don't understand the point, but Nicole gets up with her brother and drunkenly swaggers over to the barrel. They work together, the darling siblings that they are. Nicole is laughing savagely at her brother when he attempts to push it, and his hands slip and he falls. They both think this is the most amusing thing to happen all night. Their laughter is infectious. Neither one of them can stop. They finally are able to compose themselves long enough to count to three and push the huge barrel down the steps. It crashes down the steps and makes a louder bang at the bottom than I was prepared for. Lily and I watch in silence. A few moments after the barrel reaches the bottom, we hear sirens.

In reality, we all know that they are not coming for us. However, sirens to us are among the scariest sounds in the world. We leave our empties at the top and run down the steps all releasing faint screeches of terror and tugging on one another. We run until we get to a side street and begin walking quickly, all completely debilitated from our excursion.

"What do you want to do now?" Lily asks.

"I don't wanna go home yet," says Thomas.

"Hey, let's go wake Pat up," says Nicole.

"That is really, really far you, guys," I say. Lily agrees.

"Well, what else are we gonna do?" Nicole adds.

So we all agree to walk all the way to Pat's house. It's like a twenty-five-minute walk, and we have no radio. We walk with quick paces and a permeating silence.

When we arrive, the nervousness that has left my being for the last few hours has returned. There is always a scariness that is aroused when we wake up someone else. What if his parents wake up? I volunteer to stay in the street while Nicole goes and knocks on his window. Lily seconds my request to stay behind. Thomas and his sister walk to the front gate, quietly lifting up the cold metal latch with steady hands as they slip from our view. Lily and I crouch down in the street peeking through the bushes, hoping to see that the three of them have made their stealthy exit. After quietly looking through the window of branches that the bush has provided for us, Lily and I revert to our most cherished position, Indian-style. I tell Lily that it was kind of a silly idea for us to walk all the way to Pat's house because now we can't even stay that long. (Everyone knows my mom wakes up at 4:30 AM for work, and I have to be home a decent amount of time before that so that her internal clock doesn't have a chance to wake her up a few minutes early.) I talk confidently and as if I am merely reciting important facts. However, in reality, my calmness of before has all but diminished. I am shaking because I'm scared of my mother's disapproval. I say disapproval because that's what scares me more than anything.

My mother has always loved me in a very intense but tough love kind of way. I am not scared of her hitting me. She hasn't done that since I was a kid, and even then it was only a little smack on my behind. I'm not even really afraid of being punished. I have been punished for a majority of this school year due to poor grades and cutting classes. What bothers me most of all is the look that splays from her eyes when she is disappointed in me. My mother is my hero. I love the way she smells; she always smells of bleach and powder, perfectly balanced. I love the way she laughs when her eyes get all squinty and her head is thrown back. I love the values that she has instilled in my brother and me. Family is constructed like a well-oiled machine. The working order of my family consists of such things as sit-down dinners, weekly chores, and a nine o'clock curfew. There will never be any dysfunction brought to our lives by her. However, as much as I love her for caring enough to have these rules, I also resent her for making them such a part of me. There are times when I want to throw those things away and not care about how she feels when I ruin the working order of things, but it is impossible. To disappoint my mother without my chest burning and wrenching is an impossible feat. I sometimes wish my mother would do something maniacal, something insane, something impossible to forgive so that I could progress with my own life and do what I want without the fear of bruising her. I know her well enough to know that she would never even do anything for her own pleasure. Every decision she makes is based on the efficacy it will bring to both my brother and my life. So when my friends and I sneak out at night, it does something to me. Whereas my friends have the slightest fear of being caught and punished, I have the fear of being brandished by my mother's discontent. This fact makes me think about every single thing I do as if it were the actual idea of "life" that I am fucking with. The importance that she places on my decisions also makes the things I'm not supposed to do more thrilling. I hate her for placing so much weight and importance on every minuscule decision I make, but I also cannot help loving her more than anyone or anything in the entire universe. My friends all love my mother too. It is entirely impossible not to love that woman. However, they do think she is too strict. They also understand the extent of how vital it is that I get home on time, and they will always make sure that they do that for me.

"Hey, here they come," I hear Lily whisper.

Her words pull me out of my daydreams. We look through the bushes and see the figures of three people. I guess they got Pat to wake up. Lily and I both stand up and await their arrival. When they get to the street, we all continue walking down the block in silence until we are away from his house. As soon as we are far away enough, I ask Thomas to tell me what time it is. He is at first afraid to look at his watch, but I remind him how important it is that I know what time it is. He cautiously peeks at his watch through weary eyes and is relieved to tell me that it is three forty-two. I remind everyone that we need to leave in about ten minutes for the long trek home.

At this, Pat gives me a scornful glance and says, "Why did you, guys, wake me up to hang out for ten minutes?"

"It was Nicole's idea," I quickly say before anyone complains about how it is me that is really causing the rush.

"Well, does someone at least have a cigarette for me?" Pat says.

Nicole says she has one more of her mother's that she was saving for the walk home.

"Come on, share it with me now. You just freakin' woke me up to hang out for ten minutes. You can at least let me have a cigarette."

Nicole agrees, and we all walk to the park down the block from Pat's house and sit in an Indian-style, converse laden circle, and share our last cigarette. We all talk quickly, relaying the evening's events, the forties, the flowerpot, and the sirens. Pat listens attentively and says we should have woken him up first. Lily reminds Pat that he was supposed to meet us there and how were we supposed to know that he wouldn't show up again. Pat says we should do it next weekend, and he promises he will wake up.

After our chat, we say goodbye to Pat and quickly begin our walk home. When we pass the food store, we grab a shopping cart and take turns pushing each other in it all the way home.

We sing a few songs, replay the most entertaining events of the evening, and wish we had a cigarette. When we pass the trailer park, we are lucky to see a suspicious looking man out front smoking. This is Nicole's department. We all watch as she approaches the man and asks him if he has an extra cigarette. Of course, he doesn't.

We continue on our path. I continuously ask Thomas to check the time. Four twelve (luckily missed four eleven by one minute, but how weird is that?), four nineteen, four twenty-four. The pulses of my heart quicken as we get closer and closer to home. As we round the corner of our block, I see something that makes me sick to my stomach. My mother's bedroom light is on. She's already awake.

Chapter 3

PUNISHED

So I'm punished again. But this time, the anger I feel toward my mother is so great I cannot even look at her. Before I even got to the door of my house, my mother was standing there waiting for me. Of course, I tried to tell her that I just went across the street to Thomas and Nicole's house, but she just stood there shaking her head. This was an indication that she had already called their parents as soon as I wasn't in my bed. But you see, Thomas and Nicole aren't punished. Their parents just attributed their behavior to normal adolescent curiosity. But my mother believes that Thomas and Nicole do the things they do, precisely because their parents have that exact reaction. Lily got off easy because she was sleeping over at Thomas and Nicole's, and of course, Thomas and Nicole's parents aren't going to call her parents, although I'm pretty sure she would have gotten off just as easily if they had. I just don't understand why I have to have the mother I do. Why can't she see that my friends and I don't do anything that bad? We just need each other to feel alive. I know she will never understand this.

So another two weeks of punishment. No friends, no TV, no phone. So, of course, I'm going to spend my entire Saturday writing letters to my friends and leaving them in the window box attached to my bedroom window. Thomas, Nicole, and I started this tradition years ago. We both have our punishment letter spot. My letter spot is in the window box; Thomas and Nicole's are in lunch boxes that are strategically placed on the deck attached to Thomas's room. We have been doing this since we have been little children. Whether our parents have really been inobservant enough not to figure it out or they just pretend to be, I haven't yet discovered. No matter what the case, I close myself off from my mother and brother and furiously write the letters.

To: Thomas
From: Jess
Location: Hell
Time: 11:41am

Hey what's up No Frill! I seriously can't believe that my mother is being such a bitch. She makes the biggest deal out of everything. I can't take it anymore. I sometimes feel like I want to run away. Today was supposed to be a fun day and now I can't do anything because my stupid brother will tell on me if I leave the house. What are you guys gonna do today? Are you still gonna drink? I wish I could hang out. It's not fair. "I'd like to be, under the sea In an octopus' garden in the shade. He'd let us in, knows where we've been in his octopus's garden, in the shade." At least I have music to listen to. Matt would never tell on me for listening to music. Oh my goodness, oh my goodness (in "Annie" voice) what am I going to do all day? Anyway, I've been meaning to ask you. How did you know you were gay? I mean, I know you joke around all the time that I am a lesbian because I wear long shorts and Birkenstocks and am in love with Ani, but what if I am gay? How do you really know? I mean, I am definitely not attracted to girls, and I LOVE boys, especially my husband John Lennon. But how do you really know? When you say that you think I'm a lesbian are you just joking or do you see something that I don't?

Anyway, I must go now. I am bored and have nothing else to write. I guess I will just go grab some more cookies! I'm going to go write to Nicole and Lily. PLEASE WRITE BACK SOON. I am sooooo bored!

To: Lily
From: Jess
Location: Death
Time: 12:22pm

Hey what's up Lily Frilly!! Life sucks and I am so bored right now. I just wrote Thomas a letter. I miss you guys. Can you believe my mom? She is sooooo mean. It's soooo unfair. It's Saturday, and while you guys are all having fun I am stuck in here doing nothing. At least I can listen to music! Oh yea, I've been meaning to ask you. Do you have our letter notebook for school on Monday. I looked through my backpack and can't find it. I can't remember if I wrote you the last letter on Friday. I can't believe I am actually saying this but I can't wait to go back to school just so I can see my friends! It's better than being locked in here all day by myself. Ughhhhhhh.

"His sister Pam works in a shop she never stops she's a go-getter." Anyway, bored as hell but going to go. I am going to eat lunch and then I will write Nicole a letter. If she asks, tell her that I am going to write her next I promise! LOVE YOU!! BYE!

To: Nicole
From: Jess
Location: You know
Time: 1:47pm

Hey Silly Zilly!! Sorry it took me so long to write you a letter and I'm sorry that I wrote your letter last but I wanted to ask Thomas something in his letter (you can ask him to show you.) Well...I guess I will just tell you. You know how Thomas always jokes about me being a lesbian, I wanted to know why he thinks that and if he really thinks it's true. I don't think I am I just get confused sometimes. I feel like, if he is gay, maybe he knows how to detect when people are gay better than I do or something. I don't know, it's confusing. Do you think I could be a lesbian?

Anyway...enough about that. I don't want to think about it anymore. So, I just ate lunch. I made grilled cheese. Yummmmm! I also hung out with Matt for a little bit. I think he feels a little bit bad for me but he still won't let me go outside. Boo hiss! I just got the best idea! Let's all walk to school on Monday so we can hang out for a little bit before we go to school. Ask Thomas and Lily if they want to. Please please!! I am soooo lonely. Also, I have to go to all of my classes this week. I can't cut at all because if I get caught my mom is going to kill me! I seriously can't wait for this school year to be over and it to be summer again. I have to really really try to do well in school until the end of the year so I can enjoy my summer. I can't wait to go camping and go to block parties and just have fun drinking in the park and riding bikes everywhere! Ughhhhh

I just can't wait! Anyway, I am going to go now. Please write back soon I am soooo bored.

Today was the most boring day ever. Saturday nights, we usually eat a family dinner and rent a movie from Blockbuster. Even though hanging out with family is appropriately cheesy, I actually enjoy Saturday nights. However, I doubt I will be allowed to join my mom and brother tonight anyway. You know what, even if she does let me come out of my room, I'm not going to. I'm going to show her that I don't need her and that I can have fun without her. Maybe if I just keep ignoring her, she will eventually give in and talk to me or apologize or something. Yea, right. I know that's not going to happen.

Anyway, I just checked my mailbox for the sixth time today and *finally* received a letter.

To: Bill
From: Zill, Lil, No Frill
Location: Across the Street
Time: 3:00pm

Hey Billy girl!!!!! We all miss you sooo much! Don't worry, we didn't end up drinking today without you. My mom warned us that after last night she was going to tell my father if she caught us doing anything bad. We spent the entire day at my house hanging out. We stuffed our clothes with pillows and clothes again…like seriously more than ever……and walked around the house and crashed into each other! It was sooooo funny! You should have seen me (No Frill/Thomas) and Lily crashing into each other and fighting. They filled my clothes up first and I was bigger than I have ever been. Once I fell down I could not get up and Lily and Nicole starting tickling me and I actually peed in my pants. Hahahaha. My mother was just ignoring us all day and calling us assholes. Then when they were tickling me, I was screaming for my mom to make them stop and she came in the room and started tickling me too! It was insane. Anyway, they are both sitting next to me right now and they say, "Hi!" Well, that was pretty much all we did today. Oh no wait... they are telling me to tell you about the attic. We also went into the attic today and searched through all these bags and boxes of clothes that have been up there forever. A lot of the stuff was weird clothes from when we were babies or little kids, but we also found some really cool clothes of my parents from when they were teenagers. We took a few pair of really cool bell-bottoms, and Lily and Nicole took some of these weird peasant top thingy's (that's what my mom called them.). We also found some t-shirts from when we were little that look really cool again, like if we wear them in a funny way. We will show you on Monday. You should come over really early Monday before school and maybe you can wear some of the clothes we found. The bell-bottoms are so cool and we are just going to trade them every day so that we all have a chance to wear them. Hooray!!! Oh yea!! We will definitely walk to school on Monday so that we can hang out. Keep writing letters and so will we!

P.S—Here is a cigarette that we stole from my mother. MISS YOU!!!

As I lay in bed Saturday night, reading this letter for the mil-lionth time, I am missing my friends so much. I want to be with them and laugh my free-spirited, squinty-eyed laugh. I want to rem-inisce about funny memories and create new ones. I want to listen to music and figure out what the lyrics are saying together. I am going to bed early tonight, and I will probably fall asleep easily, knowing that I won't be awakened by a knock at the window.

When I wake up Sunday morning, it is to the smell of coffee and eggs. I think about how weird that is, considering that my mom is at work. Soon after I open my eyes, I hear a small tap on my bedroom door.

"Hey, Jess, you up?" comes my brother's voice.

"Yea, I just woke up," I respond.

"I made some eggs for breakfast and a pot of coffee if you want to come hang out for a bit."

I know that although Matt is generally pretty content being by himself, he does get lonely from time to time. I also know that he loves me very much, and I am his best friend.

"Okay, give me five minutes," I say and am actually excited to have someone to talk to.

I stretch quickly and turn off the radio next to my bed that has been on all night. I hate to say goodbye to Jane's Addiction, but I am actually really hungry. As soon as I step out of my room, I realize that my brother has already set a plate for me. He has made me scrambled eggs, bacon, buttered toast, and a huge cup of coffee. I know it isn't much, but I am excited about this meal before me right now. I grab the coffee, put some milk and sugar in it, and come sit back at the table where Matt is sitting across from me already eating.

After a few moments, he breaks the silence with, "Why do you have to go sneaking out at night with your friends? Can't you just stay in your bed like a normal person?"

If it was anyone else that asked me that question, I probably would have gotten angry. However, I know that this is just Matt's way of starting a conversation, and he's not trying to upset me.

Matt has always been an introvert. He has never made any close friends because of it, so he doesn't really understand what my friends and I have. He is very shy and has been known to get up and walk away right in the middle of a conversation with someone new if he is uncomfortable. For as long as I can remember, there has been a piece of Matt that has remained very distant, even to our family. He doesn't talk about things that bother him or anything even remotely resembling a feeling. For years, I thought that he was hiding something. He must be right. How can a person not have anyone to share their feelings or thoughts with? I had harassed him about it for so long until I just had to give up and realize that this is just who he is. I have realized that the way my brother shows his love is by doing kind things that he really doesn't need to do for others. If he's cooking something for himself, he will gladly make a bit more for you without anyone asking him to. He will buy the family amazing presents, and he always says yes whenever I ask him to borrow anything. He will let me borrow his favorite CD, shirt, or even money without batting an eye. These are all wonderful Matt qualities. However, if you ever ask him how he feels about something, don't expect any type of answer. My mom says that Matt is very much like my father. I wouldn't know.

"Why, Jess?" My brother's words snap me back.

"What?" I ask, not remembering what we were even talking about.

"Why do you have to keep sneaking out at night?" he asks again.

"Matt, it's really not even a big deal. My friends and I just hang out. It's fun to go out at night and walk around. It's not like we are even doing anything bad. All of my friend's parents don't make such a big deal about it. Mommy is just crazy and too strict."

"What did you do when you snuck out?" he asks.

"We just walked around. We went to the high school and sat on the steps and talked."

"Were you drinking?" he asks. I can't even hide my smirk.

"Well, yea, but we were just hanging out. It really is not even a big deal. We are teenagers. All teenagers drink. We were just hanging out and talking. Why is that so bad?" I mumble while shoving another forkful of eggs into my mouth.

"Well, for one, you are lucky that Mom had no idea that you were drinking, or you would be in even bigger trouble. But can you just try to lay low for a while and not get into any trouble? You are really killing her with all of this stuff you keep doing lately."

"Well, obviously I have to since I am punished and can't see my friends anyway," I sullenly respond.

"Anyway, thanks for breakfast. It was really good. Also, the coffee is great. Thanks. I'm going to go hang out in my room for a little bit."

I excuse myself and return to my chamber. I immediately turn the radio back on and pull out my pen and paper and begin writing notes to my friends.

Chapter 4

BACK AT SCHOOL

I made it through the weekend avoiding my mom and brother. I spent most of the time in my bedroom thinking, writing, eating, sleeping, and listening to music when my mom wasn't around. It was insanely boring. Needless to say, I am very happy it's Monday. I'm up before the alarm due to all the sleeping I did all weekend. I pretend not to rush until my mom leaves for work. As soon as her car pulls away, I get ready as fast as I can without caring much about my outfit. I'm going to change as soon as I get to Thomas and Nicole's. I apply Lily's blue mascara and watermelon lip gloss and head across the street.

I walk right in and don't see anybody. I head straight back to Thomas's room and find Nicole and Thomas taking turns spanking Lily's ass and talking about how good it looks in her jeans. Lily is just laughing and saying how happy she is that she has finally found a pair of "good butt jeans." She thanks them, but I can tell she barely believes it. That is one of my favorite "Lily qualities." She truly doesn't know how amazingly beautiful she is. Unlike Thomas and me with our mousy brown hair, she is a true brunet. Her hair is perfectly shiny and straight, and it matches her almost black-brown eyes. She has the most perfect skin that any of us have ever seen.

Almost a direct contradiction to Lily's dark features are Nicole's. Nicole is a perfectly petite blonde with beautiful but eerie blue "witch eyes," just like her mom. Thomas and I usually pass for siblings unlike him and Nicole who actually are related. Thomas and I both have the exact same skin tone, mousy brown hair color, brown eye color, and Converse size. It doesn't bother me now that people think we are related, but it used to bother me a great deal years ago when we were "dating" and everyone thought Nicole was his girlfriend when the three of us were together because they look so incredibly different.

"Hey, Jess!" Nicole yells and jumps on me with her legs wrapped around my torso.

"Hey, guys," I excitedly respond.

"We missed you so much this weekend. It was so boring without you," Nicole says after she finally jumps off.

"Do you have any clothes for me to borrow?" I ask.

Thomas tells me how he just picked up *12 Bar Blues*, Scott Weiland's first solo album, which was just released. He says I must hear it. He puts it on, then throws me a pair of amazingly cool vintage bell-bottoms and a tie-dye shirt. Lily explains how they all fought over the shirt but decided that I should wear it on Monday because I had such a terrible weekend, and it would look cool with my Hawaiian lei that I have insisted on wearing to school every day for the past month. Thomas then explains how we all need to "shut up" and listen, I mean, really listen to "Barbarella" because it is *amazing*. We do shut up. It is amazing. It makes my inside smile and glow.

After about a minute Thomas and Nicole's mom comes in and tells us to "turn down the fucking music, it is too early for that shit." After she sees me, she gives me a hug and tells me that my mom is too uptight and that she missed me this weekend. I tell her that I know my mom is the meanest most uptight woman in the world and that I missed her too. I secretly wish she was my mother. Due to my rough weekend, Leanne, Thomas, and Nicole's mom rewards me with a Marlboro Light 100's. I tell her she's the best, and I mean it.

Our walk to school is the most fun I've had since being caught. We share a few cigarettes, pass around a thermos of coffee, and we each talk about our weekends. We decide to walk through the Dollar

Store where the old Woolworths used to be. Thomas pretends not to be looking where he's going and walks right into a rack of T-shirts and knocks the whole display on the ground and falls on top of it. I laugh so hard—I have to desperately fight to catch my breath. Nicole then takes a bottle of laundry detergent and dumps a huge glob of it right on the floor.

She then begins skating around in it. Thomas sees what she's up to and again pretends to be walking along and slips in it and falls onto the floor with an impetuous screech. This time, one of the workers walks by to see what's going on. Lily and I are hiding in the neighboring aisle clinging onto each other's arms and fighting to contain our laughter. Thomas, with a perfectly straight face, tells the employee that he was walking and slipped on the detergent. Nicole is nowhere to be found. I can tell by the employee's face that he doesn't believe a word of what Thomas has just told him. Thomas walks over to us, and we all walk toward the exit. Thomas is looking at us incredulously and saying, "Can you believe I fell?"

As soon as we get outside, we notice Nicole has already made her way out here.

The rest of the walk to school we just laugh and give each other piggyback rides. When we pass the trailer park, we find a shopping cart out front. I run and jump in, and Nicole starts running, pushing, and hollering. I slump down on my knees, and with my head erect, I furiously quote Ace, "Oh, you, pretty chitty bang bang, chitty chitty bang bang, we love you." Thomas and Lily remain behind arguing about something. They are probably arguing about their failed love.

Two weeks pass until I get the courage to sneak out again. Although I know I am on thin ice with my mom, I also know that her schedule as a nurse and single mom leave her completely exhausted, and when she goes to bed at night, she is done for. My mistake last time was getting home too close to her rising time. I believe that there is a much better chance of her catching me closer to when she goes to work than soon after she goes to bed. I am convinced that this is how it works, and this is what I must believe in order for me to get the freedom I need.

I wait two Fridays from the one when I was caught. The last two weeks have been torture, but I have proven to my mother that I am "on the right track" by being there when she gets home from work every day (I had to after the scary notes she left), completing all of my homework (I had nothing else to do), and pretty much not mentioning my friends in her presence (she takes the phone to work with her and doesn't put it back on the hook until I go to bed at night). Needless to say, I have been trying to get back on my mother's good side.

Truthfully, I feel torn. There is a part of me that desperately yearns for the comfort of my mother's company. I just don't know how to do it. It doesn't feel the same as it used to. I want to bake Christmas cookies with her as we blast Mariah Carey's "All I Want for Christmas is You" and dance around the kitchen in our pajamas with smiles smeared across our flour- and chocolate-stained faces, just like the cartoonish over accentuated smiles in the "Black Hole Sun" video. That's what I want. I don't know how to do it and feel like me at the same time.

I hear the soft knock on my window at 11:47 PM. I pop my head out to let them know that I heard them and will be out shortly. I pull my JNCO's over my pajama pants and carefully climb out of my bedroom window, balancing out of the flower box that perfectly frames my bedroom window. Outside, Thomas, Lily, and Nicole await my arrival to normalcy. I quickly slip through the window and quietly stride to where they are all standing. We all walk to "The Pines" and sit in our tightly wound Indian-style circle.

I have talked everyone into staying close to home this time. Thomas has even talked his mom into buying beer for us after tirelessly performing random household chores. Nicole returned bottles and cans with Lily to make money to buy the beer. I am extremely grateful, especially since we don't have to waste time waiting at 7-Eleven asking strangers to buy us beer again.

As soon as we sit down, the fizzing that escapes from my friends' bottles, loudly at first, and then almost muted, is a welcome invitation for me to do the same. I twist off my wide mouth, and we all clang our bottles together and take that long-awaited first sip. Thomas leans over and presses play. Our Lady Peace's "Clumsy" begins. Lily pulls a pen out of her pocket and begins to draw on the side of her sneaker. I feel in my pocket, remembering the iced tea mix I have in there in a plastic baggie. I lick my finger and insert it into the baggie and pull out my iced tea laden fingertip only to pop it back into my mouth. Thomas takes out his brown leather journal with his favorite expertly chewed pen and begins to do what he always does. Thomas is able to make magic spurt from his pen while documenting this perfectly ordinary moment in time, somehow making it magical. After sharing in my powdered iced tea addiction and passing the bag to Lily, Nicole pulls out a cigarette, lights it, and exhales slowly. I untie my glittery shoelaces and retie them several times before asking Lily to borrow her pen. I draw a peace sign on the top of my white Converse drawing palette. We are all just enjoying the quiet and each other's company.

After spending so much time alone, you would think that this quiet would yank at the parts of me that yearn for the voices of my friends, but it doesn't. It is nice to just exist with these people who are a part of me. I feel calm and happy and whole. The music fades in and out of my attention. I hear some of it, but the rest of the time, I just exist.

We all finish our forties about the same time. We briefly discuss what we should do now. Nicole says that she wants to go to sleep. They all say that I should come over and sleep for a bit, and then go home in a few hours. This proposition sounds lovely, but I think I should go home. We all get up and walk back toward home. At the corner we say our goodbyes, and Thomas grabs my empty bottle to put on the side of his house with the rest of the recyclables. I tell them that I will see them tomorrow.

I climb back inside, leaving my window open a crack. I always sleep better with the cold air from the night blowing on my face. The outside air is a reminder that the world in which I belong is just outside of my window, and I can always escape into her arms if I ever need to.

I slip off my pants and climb into bed. I turn on the radio and drift into sleep with a subtle smile playing on my lips.

Chapter 5

BIRTHDAY PARTY

School is torture. The only thing that keeps me going are the looks that Thomas and I are giving each other during our Friday end-of-school assembly where we are both carefully picking single stray strands of hair from this girl sitting in the seat in front of us. It is hysterical how her hand keeps shooting up to her head, itching and looking around. It is a struggle to remain serious when she keeps turning around and desperately searching for the culprit.

I'm not even really paying attention to what this assembly is about. The importance of Regents exams, how we need to go to bed early, eat a good breakfast, take our time, don't leave anything blank, and how we will lose no points for guessing. Blah blah blah. I'm always restless and bored at these assemblies, but today I am more restless than ever, seeing that it's my birthday, and my mother is having a little "get together" with my friends after school. I am probably more nervous about this than I have been about anything in a long time. I tried to tell my mother that I didn't want a party or anything to celebrate my birthday; however, she insisted and said, "Jessica, it's not a party. It's a get-together. They're different."

So after school today, eight of my friends are coming over. My mom is getting pizza for us, and we are just going to "hang out."

However, if I know my mother, she is going to get cake, make my friends sing, and put up stupid streamers and balloons. So embarrassing. Anyway, I don't really care about Thomas, Lily, and Nicole obviously, since they are over at my house all the time and know how lame my mother is. I am just embarrassed about some of my friends from school who have never been over before. I just can't wait until it's over.

As soon as the assembly ends, I hear Thomas yelling through a group of people, "Jess!" I push through the people, all seeming to be walking in different directions.

"Let's go wait outside on the island. I told Lily earlier today to meet us there after school."

"What about Nicole?" I say.

"She'll figure it out."

"That's not nice. We should go find her."

"Jess, calm down. If she doesn't find us in the next few minutes, she'll just go to the island."

"Okay" is all I can say. I'm sure he's right.

We make our way to the island across the street from school so that we are not "smoking on school grounds." Thomas takes one of Leann's cigarettes from his lunchbox, lights it, inhales like his life depends on it, exhales steadily, repeats, and then hands it to me.

"So, are you excited about your birthday party?"

"Ughhhhhh. It's not a birthday party. I didn't even want to have anything my mom is making me."

"Your mom is trying to do something nice for you. I love your mom. We're just gonna hang out like we normally would at my house."

There he goes again with the loving-my-mother thing. I had to defend myself.

"Actually, it's going to be nothing like just hanging out at your house because we can't have a cigarette if we want to or drink or curse or do anything. It's going to be so lame."

"Damn, Jess, just chill out. Your mom is trying to be nice. Just try to have fun."

Before I can complain anymore, I spot Lily and Nicole crossing the street and making their way over here. I decide to shut up for the time being. While I'm thinking about how much I am dreading today, Nicole runs over and jumps on me. Like completely jumps on me, legs wrapped around my torso, and kisses me all over my face. I'm laughing hysterically and trying to tear her off of me and wipe off her birthday kisses.

We decide to gather the birthday guests on the island and all walk back to my house together. It ends up being only seven of us because CJ has to babysit his nieces or something. So Thomas, Lily, Nicole, Pat, Jan, Emma, and I begin our trek to the house of doom. Although my insides are writhing, the walk makes me feel better. We talk about school drama, plucking hair out of strangers' heads, and our annual camping trip. Our nonchalant conversation puts me in a good place so that I can get through the upcoming festivities.

As we near my house, my apprehension ignites again as we turn the corner to my house, and I see the streamers and balloons hanging from the umbrella on the back patio table. I am upset about these obnoxious decorations until I see that they are in my favorite colors, yellow and orange. My mom tries so hard. The thought of her at the store picking out these items in order to make me feel special on my birthday suddenly fills me with sadness. I feel so bad for the way that I treat her and all the shit that I put her through. She tries so hard to do whatever she can to make me happy, despite the fact that I have messed up so many times and am so unappreciative.

My mom looks so excited when she spots me. She analyzes my face in order to determine if I'm pleased and if what she did for me is okay. The look on her face is desperate. I have to let her know that it's okay. I smile and I don't have to fake it.

"How's the birthday girl?" my mother says as she grabs me and gives me a hug and kiss. "I already ordered pizza. I'm gonna pick it up in about ten minutes. You, guys, can just make yourselves comfortable. I have soda and stuff in the fridge too. If there's anything you, guys, need, just give a holler." She really is trying.

"C'mon, guys. Let's hang out over here. I'll be right back. I'm gonna go get my radio and the soda. Does anyone need to go to the bathroom or anything?" I lead my friends to the table with the streamers and balloons, trying incredibly hard not to blush.

As soon as I get into my room, my heart begins to beat out of my chest. Why in the hell did I agree to this? This was the worst idea ever. If I can just make it through the next few hours, everything will be okay. I never have to agree to something like this again. I flip through my CD book, thinking of what we should listen to. I settle on Sublime for now—everyone likes Sublime. I take one last long breath and head back outside. I look at my friends sitting around the table, laughing and relax a bit. Maybe this won't be that bad.

I forget about being embarrassed, nervous, and cranky. I am able to laugh with my friends, sing. I sit on Pat's lap for a good ten minutes, which I secretly enjoy. After that, I nervously get up when I think my mom might be coming back soon. Although I don't explain this to him, I just tell him he's bony and my ass hurts.

Pat is the first guy I've liked in years. I have loved Thomas since we've been kids. He was my first kiss, my first boyfriend, and my best friend. It didn't help that our parents always said, "Thomas and Jess are gonna get married someday. You just wait and see." When he and Lily first started hanging out when they were in eighth grade and Nicole and I were in seventh, I was forced to hate her. I was insanely jealous of this beautiful new girl who was taking my best friend away. Their friendship kept me up at night and forced me to harbor negative and hateful feelings toward another person besides my father for the first time in my life. Lily helped me to realize what jealousy feels like, and it ate at me for a very long time. However, despite the fact that I was unbearably and disgustingly cold toward her, gave her and Thomas dirty looks as they held hands, and drunkenly informed her that I didn't think her and Thomas made a good couple, she still attempted to befriend me in the most honest and true way. We got to know each other more and more, only due to the fact that we saw each other every day while she and Thomas were together. But the closeness that we have now was created through both a drunk sneak out night and a breakup.

Thomas, Lily, Nicole, and I were drinking forties up at the trailer park in our neighborhood. We went there to hang out with some friends from school, but they never showed up. So the four of us just stayed there and sat on the benches at the entrance and drank. The people who live there are extremely accepting of loudness and drinking in the middle of the night. Anyway, Lily was talking to us all about how she is so happy that she started hanging out with all of us. She was saying how she feels more like herself with us than she ever has, and she has only known us for a short while. I am not even sure where it came from, but I, all of a sudden, burst out crying. There really was nothing I could do about it. It was explosive and utterly uncontrollable. Thomas and Nicole just stared at me and asked what was wrong. Lily came over and put her arm around my bobbing shoulders. I know she was trying to be nice, but this friendly gesture made my crying even worse. I told her how I am a terrible person and how when I first met her, I hated her for stealing my friends away. I told her through my sobs that I was sorry and that I really do like her now and consider her a good friend. I told her that I was jealous of her because she was prettier than me and how no one in school has ever liked me. The only person who has ever liked me was Thomas. Anyway, I went on and on and apologized and cried like a lunatic. Lily put her arms around me and talked to me and made me feel better about all of the stupid things I was talking about. After that night, we never talked about my crying episode again. But Lily called me to hang out a few days later. Thomas and Nicole were at a family function, the first one I hadn't gone to in a while. Lily called me up and asked me if I wanted to hang out. This is when we hang out without Thomas and Nicole for the first time ever. Since then, we have been inseparable. After she and Thomas broke up, we became even closer. We spent many drunk, crying nights together— her about Thomas, me about how no one at all will ever like me and how everyone thinks I'm a lesbian because I never "hookup" with anyone. To say the least, this is how we got closer. I really grew to love her and still do.

For a very long time, I wasn't interested in anyone. However, Pat has shown some interest in me lately, and I really can't deny that I like him. He is so cute, always smells nice, listens to all the same music as me, always makes me laugh, and asks me if he can earn a quarter all of the time, which in our language means that he wants me to kiss him. Anyway, sitting on his lap truly solidified my feelings for him. I guess I am starting to like him as more than a friend.

"Hey, guys, I am going to leave the pizza on the dining room table so the bugs don't get to it. Come in and help yourselves when you're ready." My mother's voice snaps me back to reality.

Luckily all of my friends get up and say how they are starving. This makes me happy. I would feel terrible if no one ate any of the pizza my mom bought.

As we all eat, we talk of school and friends and music and sneaking out. When Lily says she has to go to the bathroom, I quickly jump up and say that I need to go too. A few minutes before, I saw Lily and Pat talking kind of secretly, and I need to find out what they were discussing. As soon as we get into the bathroom, I close and lock the door and jump up on the counter while Lily goes to the bathroom.

"What were you and Pat talking about before?"

Lily smiles and says, "He told me that he really likes you and wants to ask you out. He asked me if I thought you would say yes."

"Oh my goodness, my insides are all fluttery and excited, but also a little scared."

"Well, do ya like him?" she asks.

I just sit and smile not knowing what to say. I am so nervous, and I don't know why. I really like Pat. I am just so nervous about actually having a boyfriend and being expected to kiss him and do other things. I haven't kissed anyone since Thomas when we were kids, and I'm afraid that maybe I forgot how, maybe I will be terrible at it, or maybe it will ruin our friendship. I have to see him all of the time. And I am terrified of what will happen if something weird happens, and I still have to see him at school.

"I don't know. I really like him. I just don't know if I want a boyfriend. We are just becoming good friends and I don't want to ruin it."

"You won't ruin it, Jess. He really likes you."

I quietly grunt, "Mmmmmm…I just don't know if I wanna go out with him."

Deep inside, I know that I really like him and most definitely want to go out with him. The real reason I am so skeptical is because I am scared.

"What am I going to tell him, Jess?"

"Just tell him that I really like him, but I don't wanna ruin our friendship."

"Are you sure that's what you want me to say?"

I hesitate and then reply, "Yes."

As we walk outside, I notice that Thomas and Emma are deep in conversation. Nicole and Jan are laughing about something. And Pat is looking at Lily and me as we walk back outside. I make eye contact with him for only a second and quickly avert my eyes. I immediately join Nicole and Jan in order to escape. I pretend to be immersed in their conversation, but I keep looking at Pat and Lily as they sit hunched over and whisper quietly on the other side of the table.

After what seems like an eternity of conversations and CD changes, my mom walks back outside carrying a Carvel ice cream cake with extra crunchies, my favorite. She plops the cake in front of me and tells my friends that it's time to sing "Happy Birthday."

"Mom, c'mon, they don't have to sing 'Happy Birthday.'" Just as these words come out of my mouth, my friends all start to sing.

My mom lights the candles and joins in. Nicole grabs me by the waist and sways with me to the obnoxious tune. I am so embarrassed, but Nicole's gesture of comfort truly helps. I keep thinking in my head that if we can only get through this, the "birthday party" will almost be over.

After everyone sings, we devour the cake. Nicole, of course, wants to smash my face in it, but I ask her nicely not to. She agrees because it is my birthday, and I should get what I want. I sit and think and wonder if my decision not to go out with Pat is the right one. Every time I look over at him, he tries to lock eyes with me. I really hope that I didn't hurt his feelings, and I hope that my decision to not ruin our friendship didn't do exactly that.

Now that everyone has left, I am happy that this day is finally over and has ended in smiles and hugs and not in disaster or embarrassment. As I lay in bed, on the edge of sleep, I am thinking about the day and Pat and my decision not to go out with him. I feel myself drifting, and then I smell her, feel her lips on my forehead, and hear, "Happy birthday, sweetheart."

Chapter 6

MEMORIAL DAY

Our friend Jan from school is having her annual Memorial Day party. I am officially off punishment and am actually allowed to go, only after her mother talked to my mother on the phone. So embarrassing. My mother thinks it's a great idea that I start hanging out with some "new friends."

As soon as we all get there, I immediately understand that her family's Memorial Day party is nothing like a party my mother would have. There are aunts and uncles, Morrissey and Grateful Dead T-shirts. The smell of stale beer breath, skin, and cigarettes permeates. As soon as we arrive, we are all given a red plastic cup, which is immediately filled to the brim. The sight of tattoos and fake red hair fills my every line of vision.

"Hey, Jess. The next time that you see your mom, you need to tell her that I love her."

This escapes from Thomas's mouth. This has completely pulled me out of where I've been. It is so weird to hear him say that. I love my mom, but to hear someone appreciate her like that is weird. She is the one who won't let me sleep over at anyone's house because she has a "bad feeling"—the one who would like to "see me get some new friends." She seriously doesn't understand what it is like to be young and have close friends. My mom has a few friends that she still talks to from high school, but they aren't really close. They go out to lunch sometimes, but that is the extent of their friendship. They don't tell each other secrets or confide in each other about their dreams or problems. I've been at these lunches, and they basically talk about work and us kids. I feel like she doesn't understand much about friendship. She doesn't understand anything.

I sit and ponder Thomas's comment for a moment. I'm still not really sure where it came from. While I'm thinking about this, The Hollies's "The Air That I Breathe" comes on, and I am snapped out. I am instantly transported to Jan's backyard with sun shoulders and beer and friends and happiness.

I feel elated. Warmth and excitement are creeping through my being. The feeling of wet jeans dragging through spilt beer on cement and cool grass is surprisingly pleasing. I feel like I could spend the rest of my life with people who talk to me the way these people do. I feel older than fourteen.

I have an entire conversation with an "aunt" named Sue. We talk about life. Aunt Sue tells me over and over again to do whatever it is that makes me happy, even if it warrants the disapproval of others. I talk about my mother. How I will never understand how I am her daughter. How we are so different. I also talk about how I am so similar to my father, although I haven't seen him in three years. I talk about lying on my brother's bedroom floor listening to old Beatles and Stones's records in the dark and silence for hours. How there is a part of my brother and me that proves that we shared a womb, but how we are polar opposites as well. I talk about how I don't fit in with my family, how I belong somewhere else. I feel that she really understands me. She talks about how she went to Woodstock when she was my age and never went back home. She talks of drugs and hugs and peace and happiness. This feels so tangible at the moment. I can run away and never go home. I can live under a bridge, in the woods, in a car. I can be happy always in the company of friends and earth and grass. This sounds feasible.

Time passes quickly. We all drink many red cups. We roll in the grass, smoke cigarettes, and sing to the classics that are blaring through the surround sound in Jan's backyard. Our eyes turn to slits, our smiles are crooked, and we are happy. I am so excited about singing karaoke with Jan's Uncle Jeff that I produce a few wholehearted excited chuckles. He asks what I want to sing. He makes it clear that he will pretty much know any song that I can possibly think of. I come up with, Joan Baez's version of, "The Night They Drove Old Dixie Down." I did not stump him. I don't think that any song has ever contained more feeling than this one at this moment. The cold grass beneath my feet, my skin smelling of sun and stale beer.

After our karaoke adventure, we make our way to Jan's side driveway. We are Indian-style again, eye's little slits. Uncle Jeff asks me if I like to party. I, of course, reply, "Yea, I loooove to party!"

He asks again, "No seriously, you like to party?"

Before I can respond, Jan's butts in, "No, she doesn't. Leave her."

I am confused by this, but don't press. We all decide to sit and smoke a bowl, a perfect invitation to summer.

This moment is pure perfection. I have a huge smile inside that I am trying to contain. Barely any talk. When we are done, we follow Jan up to her bedroom and lay on the floor. *Ziggy Stardust* plays from start to finish in what seems like moments. Not one word is uttered.

I think about my childhood. About Thomas and I, making out in a homemade limo, a shopping cart, after our "kid marriage" celebration. I think about us pretending to play the board game Memory while making out in my bedroom, fascinated with French kissing. I think of how my stomach felt the first time I saw Thomas kiss another boy. We had cut school, went to the deli, got a short Italian, bodybuilder type, to buy us beer, went to Thomas's house, drank forties, blasted Our Lady Peace, and crawled on the floor to "Car Crash." I swayed, we smoked, created pen-ink tattoos on our feet, and then Ron kissed Thomas. I don't know how else to explain this except to say that it was a perfect kiss. It was as if Thomas was waiting for him to kiss him forever. I don't even know how you would describe a perfect kiss, but this was it. It was beautiful. It was genuine. It meant more than anything I have ever done in my life. I had never fully experienced jealousy until that moment. Since witnessing this moment, I have been waiting to have a moment like this with someone.

When Ziggy's adventure finally ends, the silence that has stretched across the room has dissipated. We drowsily walk downstairs right in the middle of Fleetwood Mac's "Gypsy."

"Hey, Jess, you sleepin' over?" Nicole' asks me as plop down in the grass, our obvious first stop as soon as we walk outside.

"Yea. My mom talked to Jan's mom yesterday."

"Do you think we could sleep over too?"

"Probably, just go ask Jan."

"No, you ask her, she's more your friend than mine," Nicole replies.

"Okay. I'll go ask her."

Jan is perfectly fine with this, and so is her mom. Soon after this invitation is made, we all climb upstairs, clothes still on, and climb in Jan's monstrous bed. Thomas and Lily somehow end up on the floor with this giant blanket with a picture of a horse on it covering them entirely. I always wonder why it seems that everyone else falls asleep so much faster than I do. I lay here for a while. I think of how happy I am, how warm, how peaceful. Then I drift off into sleep, surrounded by my best friends, completely whole and happy.

Chapter 7

KARATE

Being forced to go to karate isn't something that seems so terrible to me. However, Thomas and Nicole act as if having to go to karate is a form of torture. Lily and I have already planned to go along for the ride. Thomas and Nicole have to ride their bikes a good seven or eight miles to karate even though their mom is home. She is too tired to drive them and says they have to go or she will tell their father. I already know that we will be doing nothing more than riding bikes and possibly hanging out in the bathroom of the studio until the time when class should be over arrives.

I arrive at Thomas and Nicole's at 7:38 AM. Lily slept over again. Thomas, Nicole, and I all have bikes, but not Lily. Her little sister took hers without asking, and then got it stolen. This means she will take turns on all of our handlebars.

I am an early bird. Although being forced to wake up on Saturday morning and ride my bike to a class that I am not even attending should be an annoyance, it's not.

Thomas and Nicole spend about twenty minutes begging their mom to drive us. They complain about how far it is, how they hate karate, and how she is so mean. Nicole tries to get her to let them stay home and just not tell their dad. Nothing works. I convince them to just go.

The first few minutes of our bike trek, Nicole is pissed and seems to be on the verge of crying. After about five minutes, she is fine again. Lily is on my handlebars first. It is a beautiful June morning, and I know that it is cheesy that I'm even thinking that, but it really is. It's perfect morning-hoodie and afternoon-T-shirt weather. As we ride along, we sing our usual Beatles catalog. We distribute parts, we sing, we laugh, and we yell.

It's one of those moments when something as simple as the shadows that the trees cast on the street makes my smile stretch and my warm center burst as the liquid distributes itself throughout my body. We ride under giant oaks and maples and smell summer approaching. We finish singing, and there are a few moments of silence. It is in these moments of silence that my mind tends to wander.

As kids, Thomas, Nicole, and I would be up at six every morning of the summer. We would do the same series of things every day, always barefoot. One of our adventures was called "hopping fences." This would include hopping over the neighbors' fences in the backyards adjoining their backyard without getting caught. We would straddle the fences, land in one of the yards, and run through it to an adjoining neighbor's fence as if we were actively being chased by someone with a gun. Then we would repeat this process again and again. Another of our summer rituals was called "picking poppies." This would include sneakily picking the little buds off of the impatiens from all of the neighbor's flowerbeds, collecting them, and then having a popping celebration. We also used to just wander around the neighborhood, roaming the streets in the early morning hours. The sound of our bare feet slapping the pavement, feeling the cold in the shade and the warmth in the sun, was so inexplicably natural. Now, all these years later, there is nothing more comforting than bare feet on an early morning shadowed street.

When we get to the studio, we lock up our bikes and go right into the bathroom. We sit on the floor, and Thomas pulls out two Marlboro 100's that he stole from Leanne.

"Oh shit!" Thomas says, as he realizes that he only has one match to light. This could cause a problem if we can't get the cigarette lit before it quickly extinguishes.

"Give it to me, I will do it," I say.

I don't have many talents, but lighting a cigarette with limited resources is my forte. I quickly light the first cigarette. Thomas lights the second from my newly lit one. We are all pretty excited that we have overcome this obstacle.

"Let's faint Lily again," Nicole blurts out.

"Yes! C'mon, Lily," Thomas chimes in. "You were so funny last time. Remember you drooled everywhere."

I can't help but laugh. It was so funny.

"It was so scary last time. I don't know if I want to," Lily explains.

"Please! You are the best when you faint," Thomas childishly begs.

"Ughhhh, okay."

He can persuade her to do anything.

Lily leans against the wall. She takes about six incredibly deep breaths in and out. She finally takes one really deep breath, and Thomas put his hands around her throat and holds her against the wall. She closes her eyes. We all get silent and watch as she slides down the wall, Thomas and his grip following her down. He finally let's go as she reaches the floor. She lays there for a long thirty seconds, and then slowly opens her eyes, drool climbing over her bottom lip. As I stare at her, coming back to her senses, I swear that I hear The Verve's "Bittersweet Symphony" playing in my subconscious.

"Lily! You were drooling again!" This comes out of Thomas's mouth as though he feels Lily has no idea what's going on.

She wipes her chin with her sleeve. Nicole then jumps on her lap, laughing viciously.

"Lily, Thomas fainted you. Do you remember?"

Lily sits up slowly. "Yes, I remember. That was sooo weird. My hands and feet got all tingly. Thomas, I'm not doing it anymore. That scared me."

"That's what you say now. You will do it again," Thomas replies.

I don't say anything. I know that she will do it again if Thomas asks her to.

As soon as Lily recovers, Thomas and Nicole talk about last weekend when they went to their Aunt Delores's house. They tell the story of Leanne getting drunk, falling down the stairs, trying to say that she fell down the stairs because her heel broke, and then crying because her own family doesn't believe what she says. When they got home, Thomas and Nicole ran away to the camper on the side of their house. They slept in there. They talked about how their dad must have known they were in there and didn't say anything even though he normally would have been furious. Lily talks about how her mom, Denise, fell asleep drunk with a cigarette in her hand again. She talks about how her dad never came home and how he said he had to work late but that she knows he just didn't come home and must have volunteered to work late because he never wants to be around Denise. I just sit and listen, thinking about my last Saturday when my mother, Matt, and I sat on the couch watching *Point Break* for the millionth time, eating microwave popcorn, and imitating characters from the movie. My weekend suddenly seems insignificant.

After about an hour, a million Ace Ventura imitations, it is finally time to leave. I volunteer to take Lily on my handlebars first again. Thomas and Nicole go ahead of us and argue about her stealing his CDs without asking and getting cigarette ashes all over the covers. Lily and I straggle behind as she talks all about how much it bothers her that Thomas said that Veronica is hot. Veronica is a girl from school that we see at parties.

"I thought he was gay. How does he think she is hot? When we were together, he never even said I was pretty."

"Lily, he's just trying to piss you off."

"How do you know?"

"I can just tell."

Just as we finish this exchange, Thomas looks back and yells, "What are you, guys, talking about?"

We just start laughing so hard. I start forcing myself to laugh like I do. Pushing all of the air out of my lungs until there is nothing left. When you make yourself laugh for a good minute or so, the real laugh eventually sneaks out. Lily loses it when I do this. She starts laughing beautifully hard. I start laughing so hard that my left eye closes. I laugh until I become weak and my handlebars start to wobble.

"Ahhhhhh...I'm going to falllllll!"

Lily jumps off the handlebars just in time, and I swerve my bike onto someone's front lawn. I throw myself down and lie there laughing for what seems like ever. The children who live here peek their heads out of the window. I can't stop laughing or get up. Nicole tries to get me to stand up, and I just can't do it. I keep laughing. The woman who lives here peeks her head out of the door.

"Are you okay? What's goin' on here?"

"Nothing," says Lily.

"She just fell off of her bike, but she's okay. C'mon, Jess, get up!"

This makes me laugh even more. Thomas puts his bike down, pretends to trip on the curb, and falls on top of me. Then Nicole jumps on top of both of us, followed by Lily. We lie there in a heap, laughing, dying, forever.

Chapter 8

THE BEACH

I love the beach. I always have. There is nothing in this universe that makes me feel more free than standing where the water meets the sand and looking out at the crashing waves and the sparkling sea that extend out for what seems like forever. I love the feeling of lying in the sun after swimming in the icy waves for hours. The sun seems to drink the water right off of your skin as you lay there in the sand, giving up those droplets of water as a thank-you gift. I love the smell of the dried saltwater on my skin and the way it leaves those little white patches on your legs, a mark that you have swam in the earth's womb. If for nothing else, that's why I love this island; if for only two or three months a year, it gives me a piece of nature to fall back in love with every summer.

Today my mom is taking Thomas, Nicole, Lily, Matt, and me to the beach. I turned over this morning with a huge smile on my face when I awoke to the sound of ice being poured into our red Igloo cooler. We have had that cooler for as long as I can remember. The Igloo's first appearance of the season is like a "welcome summer" party to me. I love that cooler and all that it represents.

I jump out of bed, throw on Lily's swimsuit, and head across the street to wake up the others. Nicole has my yellow Speedo, Lily has Nicole's red one, and I have Lily's green one. I walk right through Thomas's back gate, up the deck stairs, and into Thomas's room. He is still sleeping as usual. I walk into Nicole's room, and she and Lily are passed out as well.

I bend down and whisper into Lily's ear, "Lily, wake up, it's Jess."

She opens her eyes and elbows Nicole. "Nicole, wake up, Jess is here."

Nicole grunts, "Nooo. I'm tired."

Knowing it will take me more than a shake to wake her up, I climb on top of both of them and start singing The Beatles classic, "Good morning, good morning…after a while you start to smile, now you feel cool / Then you decide to take a walk by the old school / Nothing has changed, it's still the same / I've got nothing to say but it's okay…"

"Okay, okay, I'm up. What the hell, Jess?" Nicole scratchily belts out.

I reply, "We're going to the beach remember? My mom is going to be ready to go in like ten minutes, and we still need to wake Thomas up."

"You go wake him up, let me sleep for five more minutes," Nicole scratchily begs.

I ask Lily, "Lily, please come with me to wake Thomas up."

Lily climbs over Nicole, away from her spot closest to the wall, a given, since Nicole is afraid of hands grabbing at her from beneath the bed while she sleeps. She puts on Nicole's Speedo, pulls on boxers and a T-shirt, and walks with me into Thomas's room. Lily whispers in my ear that on the count of three, we will both jump on Thomas until he wakes up.

"One, two, three."

We vigorously jump on top of Thomas, laughing hysterically as Thomas moans and sticks his head under the blanket. Lily jumps off of the bed, grabs at the corner of his blanket, and begins yanking the blanket off. Thomas grabs at the blanket, attempting to keep it at all costs. I climb over Thomas and grab onto the blanket with Lily. After a few good tugs, we are successful. Thomas pretends to still be asleep.

Cocoa, the bear that Lily gave him years ago, is pulled close to his chest. Lily goes in, grabs at Cocoa, and starts to pull.

"Noooooooo," Thomas groans.

"Thomas, get the hell up. We have to go to the beach," Lily says.

He opens his eyes, but a look of wretched crankiness resides on his face. "I'm tired."

"I know, Thomas, but my mom is leaving soon. Get up!"

"Okay, okay." Thomas slowly sits up, still clinging to Cocoa.

He yawns, gives us both a look, and stands up. Without saying anything, he grabs his bathing suit from the floor and brings it to the bathroom to change. We go back to Nicole's room and sit on the edge of her bed and begin to bounce ever so slightly, just enough to make her uncomfortable. To our surprise, Nicole gives us a look and quickly gets out of bed and slips right into her bathing suit. Nicole sneaks into her mother's room, grabs three cigarettes out of her mother's pack right off of the end table, without her mother even stirring.

"Nicole, are you going to tell your mom that you are going to the beach with us?" I ask.

"No, it's okay," Thomas replies.

Then without another word he goes to the kitchen and begins scrawling a note to his mother, which he leaves on the table.

Within minutes, we are racing down the causeway in the back of my mother's car, windows open, radio blasting. We tell her to put the radio louder. It is difficult to hear over the wind. Because it's "Classic Rock," my mom lets us blast Fleetwood Mac's "Seven Wonders." Nicole, like the rest of us, loves Fleetwood Mac, so she makes it her purpose to dramatically lisp all of the "S" as loudly as she can. I am laughing hysterically and making my Jim Carey smile where my neck bulges. Nicole then starts leaning to the left, and then to the right, trying to make us all wave in unison. After five seconds, we recognize her purpose and sway along in a wave together. Matt looks back over the front seat, gives us a smile, and continues staring straight ahead. By the time we get to the second bridge, the smell of salt water races up my nostrils and forces the curves of my mouth to reach for the edges of my eyes.

When we get to the beach, we follow my mother's strict routine and lay the sheet out, put the cooler on one corner, the beach bag on another, our flip-flops on the third, and the remainder of our belongings on the fourth. My mother likes things done neat and orderly. As soon as we get the "okay," we tear off our outside clothes and run down to the water. I don't even stop running. As I get closer, I begin to scream and continue as I run directly into the waves and dive under the water. Once I go under, I begin to coax my friends to come in. It takes them a little while, but soon we are all in. We float with our heads facing away from the waves and laugh as we each get blasted unexpectedly. We ride waves in, laughing as the swirl around our feet drags us below as we get closer to shore. Then we decide to sit in the sand at the shore and repeatedly get smashed by waves, laughing as each of us fights to find the surface. After a good hour or so in the water, we decide to go back to the blanket and dry off in the sun. Thomas pretends to trip like three times on his walk to the blanket. I absolutely lose it as he realistically trips over his feet and lands headfirst in the sand, apologizing to those around him. It never gets old.

As I walk back up to the blanket, my mother stands up and holds out a towel. I back into it, and she wraps it around my back and rubs my shoulders gently as if to warm me up. She then does the same thing to everyone else. My mother is really very maternal.

We lay silently in the sun, our eyes closed as the sun drinks the last remnants of salt water from our skin. It feels so amazing to soak in the sun while the freezing outer layer of my skin tingles.

After some time passes, my mother offers us lunch; she has packed sandwiches for all of us. She has also packed puffed Cheez doodles, mine and Lily's favorite. We like to suck on them until they disintegrate on our tongues. We explain this process to Thomas and Nicole, and they attempt to master it. Lily and I mastered it back when I was in seventh grade, and we used to stay up all night when I slept over her house and played Super Nintendo and chain-smoked her mother's Private Stocks.

We laugh and eat and talk. When my mom goes down to the water to cool off, we reminisce about our first time smoking cigarettes on top of the camping mountain where the waterfall resides. I don't say anything to them, but I think about how that whole experience made me feel like I was growing up.

After a little while, we go back in the water. We sit toward the shore with our backs facing the waves again so that they creep on us and swirl and pound us into the shore. We sing Ani's "Swandive," not altering our language for the small children who are around.

After getting back to the blanket and repeating the process several times, it is time to go home. The car ride home is much quieter. We are all tired from giving our bodies and souls to the sun and waves for the day. Nicole lays her head on my shoulder, and Lily and Thomas hold hands. The Verve Pipe's "The Freshman" plays quietly in the background.

Chapter 9

SNIPPET

Sometimes I am just sad. My eyes can cry at any moment. Life seems a terrible place. I feel the unfairness of living a life where no one but my family loves me. I really do want to have a boyfriend who finds my quirks becoming, who can listen to a song and feel it like I do, who can roam the earth in bare feet and talk with me and realize how amazing it is to just walk. Why can't I find someone? I know that I am not as beautiful as Lily or that I don't have the fearlessness that Nicole has, but is there really no one that I can connect with? No one deserves me if they can't feel "Free Fallin'" like I do.

I have always loved Poe's poem "Alone." As close as I have always felt to my friends, there has been a part of me that has remained alone. It's that human desire that I have to form a connection with someone in the same way that Thomas and Lily are connected. What it would be like to have someone to understand my silence, someone who really thinks I'm beautiful, someone who, as long as they were with me, would be fulfilled.

I am lying here on my bed, listening to Counting Crows. Listening to music from middle school, from a time when life was simpler, always provides me with a certain tranquility.

There is one half of me that feels numb and in peace and another part of me that constantly longs. Who am I and what am I here for?

I feel like I could run away right now: on foot, bike, love, whatever. As long as I had music I would be okay. I don't really know where I would go, but I know there would be bare feet and grass and laughter and smiles and music. And maybe even water. Not like from a faucet, but from a waterfall or a river or something of the sort. I know that, that would make me truly complete.

I miss my dad. He was such a part of my life until a few years ago. Another divorce and another person that he let me get close to is gone. It makes me so mad that I actually care. I wish that I could just forget about all of it and move on with my life and act like it isn't a big deal. I begin writing furiously on my lily pad notepad.

Hey Dad. Although you haven't been physically, tangibly there for a lot of my teenage years, you have always been here with me. As much as I have always wanted to fight the part of myself that contains you, I have come to realize that you are very much a part of who I am. From a very early age, music moved me in a way that was almost eerily too powerful. Lyrics have a way of taking over my body. They make me cry and smile and sway. I know that this is a part of me that came from you. Mommy has told me a million stories of you listening to records for hours down in the basement, tuned to maximum volume. She also told me about how when John Lennon died, you walked around carrying his picture and crying for days. This is a part of you that I understand completely.

I stop here. I don't know what else to write, and I have nothing else to say, for now. I don't even know why I am sad. I have a great family and the best friends in the world. Sometimes I just get into these weird moods, and I'm not even sure why.

Tomorrow we are leaving for our annual Memorial Day camping trip. I guess I will just immerse myself in packing.

Chapter 10

CAMPING

I wake up with a smile plastered to my face this morning. In just a little while, we are leaving to go camping for Memorial Day weekend. Mr. Rosetti said that we are leaving at 9:00 AM on the dot so I need to be there no later than 8:45 AM.

I roll over, the remnants of my camping-induced smile lingering. I look at the clock, and it reads 8:11 AM. No time to freak out about "The Eleven Disease" right now. In actuality, it does freak me out a bit, but I have no one to share my fears with so I just try to ignore it.

My bags are all packed so I am going to just wash up quickly and head to the Rosetti's.

As I walk in the front door, I can hear Mr. Rosetti already yelling at Nicole, "Get the hell up, we are leaving in ten minutes."

I walk to Thomas's room and immediately see Lily sitting on the edge of his bed watching him do some last-minute packing while Semisonic's "Closing Time" fills the space. Nicole is cursing and grunting from her room. It sounds like she finally got up and is throwing stuff into a duffel bag.

I jump up next to Lily and immediately feel comfort. Thomas and I have talked about this before—being with Lily in any capacity brings immediate comfort. She is such a calming force that if I were ever to be put in an uncomfortable situation of any kind, I would want Lily to be by my side.

After sitting and waiting for Thomas and Nicole to finish packing, Mr. Rossetti, Leeanne, and the rest of us all drag ourselves to the van and sit in our usual spots and get comfortable, knowing that we intend on sleeping most or all of the way upstate.

I'm not sure how long I have been sleeping. I am still drowsy, and my eyes remain closed. But I can hear, from what seems like so far away, Thomas and Lily whispering to each other. I can't really make out what they are saying, but they must be awake. I slowly open my eyes and turn in their direction.

"Hey, Jess" Lily sleepily says when she notices me looking in her direction.

"Where are we? Are we close?" I sleepily ask both of them.

"We passed Custard's Last Stand a little while ago so I think we are getting close. Dad, how far are we?" Thomas drowsily inquires.

"Close. About twenty more minutes," he replies.

"Can you put on Fleetwood Mac please?" Thomas asks his dad.

It's one of the things that we all can agree to love, and his parents can deal with us listening to. Without a complaint, his dad pops in *Tango in the Night* and "Big Love" begins dancing in our ears.

We listen methodically, our knees resting on the seats in front of us. We look out the windows. Thomas and Lily exchange small words with one another every few minutes, but I have no idea what they are talking about.

We turn into the campground, and I immediately remove my knees from the seat back, sit up straight, turn around, and push Nicole in the arm in order to wake her up.

"Nicole, wake up, we are here."

She surprisingly doesn't argue. She sits up, rubs her eyes, and pushes her pillow next to her.

The van rolls down the steep hill that leads to Thomas's uncle's plot of land. The anticipation and excitement begin to take over.

As soon as the van comes to a stop, we take turns, crouch out of the van, do a quick stretch, and walk over to the river to make sure that it still exists in all of its glory. We immediately help to unload the van. Although I know that we all want to complain about this immediate expectation of work, none of us complain, because we know that the sooner we help to set up, the sooner we can wander off.

After about an hour, Mr. Rosetti finally gives us the okay to wander off for a bit. We don't even have to ask each other where we are going to go. We have done this so many times. We drag our camping-worn, Converse-laden feet off of Thomas's uncles property and start our trek up the dirt road that leads to the path where we can head up the mountain to our spot. As soon as we are out of vision, I run in front of everyone and start screaming, "I've got fidgety feet…" Nicole runs up to me and jumps on my back. I keep running and singing. Thomas and Lily are straggling behind, but once Nicole and I get a little head start, Thomas yells out, "Wait up!"

Nicole, still on my back, yells back, "Hurry up!"

When we get to the path that leads up to the mountain, Nicole hops off, and we wait for them to catch up. As soon as they are close, we begin our way into the woods and follow the trodden path that eventually ends at the base of a waterfall. We then use rocks that seem strategically placed within the hills' curves as supports for our weary feet as we make our way up. We pull ourselves up big boulders and use tree stumps as leverage to continue our ascent. It's a little difficult at first, since we haven't done it in a while; the first time is always the hardest.

Nicole and I get to our spot just at the top of the waterfall first. We sit down, and Nicole instantly pulls out a pack of Reds from her sock. She takes two out, hands one to me, and takes one for herself. She lights hers, and then hands me her cigarette to light my own. It feels glorious after all these hours. Just as I take my first pull, Thomas and Lily sit down so that we create a little half circle at the top of the waterfall. Even though we have done this a million times, it never gets less amazing or peaceful to be up here. As soon as I sit down, I can feel my entire body relax.

Lily and Thomas each take a cigarette out of their sock chamber and inhale sweetly.

"What do you, guys, want to do when we get back?" Thomas asks.

"Let's go jump on the trampoline," Nicole says.

There is a trampoline on the neighbor's property from a family who lives here year-round. They don't mind us using the trampoline.

"Let's go swimming. It's still early. We can go on the trampoline tonight. Plus, I feel gross," Lily says.

"I can go swimming," I add.

It's agreed that we will go swimming.

We leisurely smoke the remains of our cigarettes. As we each breathe in our last drag and extinguish them beside our feet, their completion signifies the beginning of our weekend. I take my shoes off first. I roll up my socks and push them in the toes of my shoes. I walk over to the small pool at the top of the waterfall and dip my feet in its icy embrace. It's intensely cold, but it feels so good. I sit at the rocky edge and keep my feet beneath the icy surface.

I look over, and Thomas and Lily and Nicole are all coming over, their bare feet asking to be immersed. They step in next to me, utilizing each other's shoulders for support as their feet slip on the wet rocks.

We sit in a half moon at the top of the waterfall. Our feet are slowly becoming numb, but the small streaks of sun that have burrowed their way through the tiny openings in the leaves of the trees on the mountain are warming our shoulders and backs and souls. It isn't very often that I am able to notice the beauty in my surroundings, but right now I can. As we sit up here, at the top of this mountain, we can look over the top of it and see the water make its final splash in the pool below, throwing a misty spray out in every direction. There are green trees everywhere and the everlasting scent of muddy pine. It really is beautiful. I'm not sure if my friends are noticing the same things that I am, but we are all quiet and seem to be immersed in some sort of pondering, whether it be the beauty of our surroundings or life in general.

"My feet are completely numb, guys. Are you ready to go back?" I blurt out after a few minutes.

Everyone murmurs some sort of assent. We move over to the rocks next to the pool of water and slip our shoes and socks back on. Thomas begins making his way down the mountain and the rest of us follow. Although going down is easier in some respect, it still requires a certain amount of practiced balancing and correct foot placement. When we get to the bottom, all of us lock arms at Nicole's insistence and create a straight line as we walk back to the campground.

"Let's go put our bathing suits on so we can go swimming in the stream," Thomas reminds us as we enter the property.

Thomas walks directly into the camper to change as the rest of us go grab some water. He emerges less than a minute later, and we switch places. We change in record time, still amped up by first day of camping intoxication. Thomas is already waiting right by the stream for us. He slips slowly down the side of the muddy stream until he is in. The water reaches his midthighs. His hands are up in the air as if to warn the water not to come up any higher. His face is twisted in this hilarious grimace, and he yells out, "It's so cold, guys. I'm freaking freezing. I don't remember it being this cold."

"It's always really cold for Memorial Day, you just don't remember," Lily replies.

"Nicole, if you freaking splash me, I will drown you," Thomas continues while looking at his sister.

"I won't splash, I promise," she adds before saying, "Who's going in next?"

We all just look at each other.

"Fine, I will go," I reply, breaking the silence.

I always feel the need to be the brave one—I have no idea why. I stealthily slide down the mud side of the steam while facing Nicole and Lily, still up at the top. My mouth immediately makes an "O" as my feet, then my knees, then my thighs hit the water. It is very cold, but as I turn to look at Thomas, he already seems less cold than he did a few minutes ago. Maybe we will get used to it. I lie to the girls, just to get them in sooner and say, "It's really not that bad once you get in."

"C'mon, Lily, you go next, and then I will come in after you," Nicole says.

"Fine," Lily replies as she comes in.

She slides in backward like the rest of us did, making the same cold squeal as her limbs hit the surface, and then submerge. Lily comes over to Thomas and me. I know that it was cold, but I am actually getting used to it now. Now that the three of us are in, I guess Nicole feels like she is finally ready. She quickly glides in, but then utters a string of curse words as she wades over to the rest of us.

Now that we are all in, we decide to walk a tiny bit downstream, mostly so that we are out of earshot of the campground. We walk very slowly, our bare feet slipping on the rocks below. I am being so careful on these extremely slippery rocks, but out of nowhere I step on a pointy one that equally scares the crap out of me and hurts my arch. I jump up and scream and end up falling in the water so that the only thing sticking out is my head.

"Ow…that freaking hurt!" I yell as my head bobs above the surface, and I try with all of my might not to let the water get my head too.

Thomas immediately begins laughing at me and asking me between breaths what happened. After explaining that I stepped on a pointy rock, I am calm enough to realize that the water doesn't seem that cold now.

I decide I want to pull myself by the arms through the water while letting my feet drag behind me with my head resting on the surface of the water. I, all of a sudden, pretend that I am a dog, and I pull myself over to where Lily and Nicole are. And I begin barking up at them and nipping at their legs. They start laughing hysterically, and then Thomas comes down with me and pretends to be a dog too. We are both bobbing around Nicole and Lily and barking our heads off. I begin to laugh at this ridiculous scene as if I am watching it from above. Then Thomas begins pawing at the water and splashing Lily and Nicole while continuously barking like a mad dog. I can't stop laughing. Nicole is trying to hide behind Lily so as not to get wet, but she is pulling on her so hard that Lily loses her balance and falls down into the water with Nicole still clinging to her. Now that we are all immersed, I bark over to Nicole and Lily and splash and bark at them until they start doing it back. We are all barking and pawing and splashing at each other like maniacs. The next thing I know, I look over and see a family peeking at us at the edge of the stream. This embarrasses me at first, but Thomas starts barking even louder until the whole thing is so funny that I can't stop laughing.

When we are finally able to control ourselves enough to get up, we turn around without saying a word and begin walking back toward the campground. We are trying to go faster this time around in order to get away from the scene, so we hobble back, holding onto each other as we try to maneuver the slippery rocks beneath our feet.

When we get back to the campground, Thomas and Nicole's dad asks us to help him set up some more stuff. We help to set up canopies for shade, a kitchen area, and then we separate for a while. Thomas needs to continue helping his father set up some stuff, while Nicole, Lily, and I head to the tent. We quickly organize our things, and while we have the chance, we all snuggle under the blankets and take a nap.

I open my eyes to see Thomas snuggled in next to Lily and Nicole still sleeping with her snuggle pillow. When did Thomas sneak in here? I must have been exhausted. I peek out the window and see that it is dusk. I can hear voices talking outside. I can smell what smells like hot dogs barbecuing. I am starving, and I have to pee. I am going to head to the bathroom before I wake them up. I crawl out of my spot and down the camper steps, not really trying to be quiet. I hope that my disturbance wakes everyone up. I creep over to the woods at the edge of the campground, walk in about twenty feet, quickly look around and make sure that no one is in sight, and go to the bathroom. I walk back to the tent and unzip the door. As I look inside, everyone is awake and talking in their raspingly sleep-filled voices.

"Hey, Jess. Where were you?" Lily asked.

"I just woke up too and went to the bathroom. Are you, guys, hungry? I am freaking starving."

Everyone agrees that they too are starving.

"Okay. Jess, can you hand me my shoes? I think that they are right behind you," Thomas asks.

I hand him his shoes and tell them that I will wait outside for them.

Within a minute, the three of them hobble out of the tent, with disheveled hair and hand and pillow markings on cheeks and foreheads. I wonder if I look like this too.

"Come and eat, guys. Perfect timing," Mr. Rossetti yells over at us while handling the grill.

We all walk like zombies over to the assembly line and grab plates, buns, and forks and continue to walk down the L-shaped tables that are strewn with all sorts of camping delicacies such as Leanne's famous macaroni salad, baked beans, and all sorts of barbecued meats. We each grab heaping plates and head over to sit on the logs surrounding the fire that must have been started while we were sleeping. The sky is gradually becoming darker. We shovel food in our mouths, barely talking as the fire warms the air that is suddenly becoming slightly chilly as the sun begins to set.

After we finish eating, we continue to sit around the fire until it is completely black outside, save for the stars that are a million times brighter than at home, even though we are only a few hours away. After staring at the flames and digesting a bit, we decide to make our way over to the neighbor's trampoline. We have to walk down this pitch-black path between the two properties. We have done it a million times, and it never gets less scary; all of us spent too many years of our childhood watching horror movies. I don't think any of us have ever walked down this path at night without having an arm or hand locked with another person's. We all fight for a minute because I automatically grab Lily's arm; she's closest to me, but she also makes me feel the safest. Thomas complains because he wants to lock arms with Lily. Nicole says that she doesn't want to lock arms with her brother. So Nicole locks onto my arm on the outside, and Thomas locks onto Lily's arm on the other side. We are now a line of four making our way down the path.

Even as little kids, we would do the same thing. I have this memory of walking down this same path with Thomas and Nicole as little kids and us stepping with the same foot at the same time chanting, "Lions and tigers and bears, oh my!" faster and faster until we were finally running and made it out on the other side, where we could finally see the neighbor's porch light shining over the dewy grass. It's not a very long path, but I honestly wouldn't want to do it alone. Also, I lucked out this time with getting an inside spot.

As soon as the trees begin to open and we can see the yard before us, I feel Nicole let go of my arm just as I see her run ahead of us straight up to the trampoline. I unlatch myself from Lily and start running right behind Nicole. Lily and Thomas continue to walk behind us. When I get to the trampoline, Nicole has already kicked her shoes off and is bouncing up and down and laughing in her excited raspy screechiness. I roll myself into a ball and lay down on the trampoline as I become her little popcorn kernel, popping all over the place. Thomas and Lily have made it to the trampoline now, and they just sit on the side and get lightly bounced by Nicole as they sit with their feet dangling over the side. It seems that they are still immersed in one of their usual inner examinations.

Nicole eventually flops down, breathless from "popcorning" me all over the trampoline. We both lay down in the middle of the trampoline. Thomas and Lily seem to have finished their conversation too, because they both slip off their shoes, swing their feet over the side, and slide into the middle to join Nicole and me. I always find it interesting that we never need to mention how or what position we will claim. We just end up sitting in our perfect full-moon circle.

I am not sure how much time has passed, I'm guessing about an hour or two. It all started with Nicole mentioning that she hopes that her mom doesn't get drunk and have a big fall again on this camping trip. This got Thomas to talking about how a few months back, he left school in the middle of the day because he just "couldn't" go to his afternoon classes, and when he got home, his mom was passed out on the kitchen table. He said that he saw her there, got scared, and immediately ran out of the house and walked back to school without ever telling any of us. Lily then talks about how some random person from school came up to her and informed her that she saw her mom riding around their apparently shared neighborhood, drunk on a bicycle.

This conversation went around and around. I added a few snippets of sadness about my dad, but my problems suddenly seemed so miniscule. Here are these three amazing individuals, these vibrant souls, these utterly funny, kind and loyal people, and they all have these secrets at home. I feel almost ashamed that I even have the nerve to complain about my problems, when my three best friends really suffer. But again, this is why I love them. Not once have any of them made me feel silly for complaining.

We probably would have continued to talk, but the slightly damp chill of night made the idea of sitting by the fire that much more enticing. Thomas was the one who broke one of our thirty-second silences to suggest that we saunter back to our logs beside the fire. We all agree, hop off of the trampoline, and lock our elbows in one long straight line before heading back through the tree tunnel with its ominous nighttime moon-soaked canopy.

As soon as we arrive at the other end of the tree tunnel, the fire is calling us. We all take our spots, except for Thomas, who runs to get his boom box. He came equipped this time with plenty of those giant batteries that are so overpriced and, I swear, are used for the sole purpose of boom boxes. And the manufacturers know that all of us angsty teens will pay the hefty price for an hour of tunes when we really need it. Thomas sets it on the one lonely log that is across from all of us and puts on Our Lady Peace's "Clumsy."

We have talked minimally, as "Clumsy" generates an abundance of time for self-reflection and wondrous silences for all of us. As the adults stop adding more fuel to the fire, the thought of warm sweatpants and hoodies and blankets beckons us. As soon as the music stops, we all just kind of know that we are beat. Thomas picks up his boom box and heads into the camper. We all follow. I grab some water in a cup, go back outside with Lily, and we quickly brush our teeth and rinse our faces, while Thomas and Nicole get changed inside. We have a natural rhythm when it comes to doing this kind of thing. We have had a million sleepovers at this point, and we both are quite similar in regard to our nightly rituals. As soon as we are done, we walk into the camper. Nicole is already what I assume is asleep with her head facing the wall on the bottom bunk. I climb in next to her and let Lily get the end. It is understood that she get the end in case Thomas hangs his hand over the side from the top bunk to hold Lily's hand as they drift off to sleep. I'm not sure if they do this tonight. I fall asleep so rapidly and deeply.

I smell bacon and coffee and hear Mr. Rosetti's strident laughter bouncing off of every piece of nature around along with the mumbling of other adult voices talking and laughing. I think his laughter woke up everyone else too, because just as I hear it, I roll over and see Lily's eyes wide open and staring straight at me. As soon as we lock eyes, we start laughing. Our laughter wakes up Thomas, who we hear turn around and grunt above us, while throatily inquiring, "What are you, guys, laughing at?"

To which Lily responds, "Your dad just laughed so loudly and ridiculously that it woke up me and Jess at the same time. You didn't hear that?"

Thomas then crankily says, "No. I just heard you, guys, laughing. I am so tired. Why did you have to wake me up?"

No one can get mad at Lily, even early in the morning. It's nice to wake up with her, and Thomas must know it, because he smiles and hangs his head over the side of the top bunk and looks down at us and gives us a hint of a sleepy smile.

"Okay. I guess I'm up anyway, and I'm starving. Lily, can you throw my pants up here?" Lily then grabs Thomas's sweatpants from the floor beside our bed and tosses them up to Thomas.

He slides them on while he is still under the covers. Nicole continues to sleep through all of this. I ask no one in particular, "Should I wake up Nicole?"

Before getting an answer, Thomas throws Cocoa over the side of the bed, right at Nicole's head. I climb out of bed right over Lily. I hate when Nicole is in a bad mood in the morning, and I don't want to hang around and wait for her crankiness. Luckily, she just grunts, "I'm already awake you, assholes," and turns over.

I slip my hoodie and Converse on, which are still damp from last night's dewy grass and head outside so everyone else has room to change. Thomas comes out to the makeshift kitchen area to join me, while Lily and Nicole get dressed. He grabs a paper plate and starts filling it with pancakes and cantaloupe; he decided that he was going to be a vegetarian about six months ago and has stuck to it surprisingly well. I grab a paper plate and fill it with pancakes and cantaloupe too, but with added breakfast sausages and bacon. Thomas waits for me to fill my plate, and then the two of us walk over to the logs by the fire. Just as we sit down, Lily and Nicole walk out of the camper and immediately walk over and grab paper plates. They fill them up and come and join Thomas and me over on the logs.

We eat in near silence, scarfing our provisions, and waking up a bit more with each passing bite. I have no idea what time it is, but based on the heavy dew that still sits on the top of the grass, along with a small wet chill in the air, I'm guessing that it is still pretty early. I wonder what time the adults woke up in order to already build the fire and make breakfast. I yell over at Mr. Rosetti who is throwing some more sausages on the grill and ask, "Mr. Rosetti, do you know what time it is?"

He looks down at his watch, and yells back over, "7:43 AM."

I have always been a bit of an early bird, so this is not that surprising for me to be up this early, but I don't think I have seen Thomas or Nicole up this early since we went camping last Labor Day.

After eating breakfast, we all decide that we would like to wash up. We put on our bathing suits, grab a towel, and stuff our toothbrushes, toothpaste, and a bottle of communal shampoo into Thomas's backpack. We throw our shoes on, and the four of us hop onto two bicycles and head back to the mountain, this time to shower at the bottom of the waterfall. I end up riding Nicole on the handlebars of her bike, while Lily plops onto Thomas's handlebars. It is a short ride up the dirt road to the waterfall, and I break the silence of the surrounding woods by huffing and puffing The Beatles "Norwegian Wood" between pedal strokes.

We arrive at the bottom of the waterfall a few minutes later, and Thomas and I stop riding, telling our passengers to get off of the handlebars. And we all walk, Thomas and I with the bikes through the woods right to where the waterfall drops into a shallow rocky pool at the base.

Thomas and I lay the bikes against a tree, and we all lay our towels and shoes on the biggest of the rocks that create a semicircle around the base of the waterfall. Thomas gets the shampoo out of his backpack, and we all submerse our bare feet into the icy pool.

"Ahhhhhhhhh! The water is freezing," Thomas yells, as he leans against Lily, who hasn't yet put her feet in.

I ignore his warning and step right in. "Oh my goodness! It is so freaking cold!" I add.

I stand there freezing, but don't get out. I know that the only way for my feet to stop tingling from this icy water is to stay in.

"Is it really that cold, Jess?" Lily asks.

"Yes, it is seriously freezing. But we will get used to it," I try to convince everyone, including myself.

"Lily, come in at the same time as me," Nicole demands, while grabbing onto Lily's arm.

They both step in at the same time, their faces contorting into all sorts of weird displays. Soon we are all in, and since my feet have been in the longest, I am actually starting to either get used to it or I am so numb that I have stopped feeling anything at all. I trek into the pool a little deeper with Thomas trailing right behind me. When I get close enough to the base of the waterfall, where I can actually feel the spray of water leaving sprinkles on my skin, I stop and turn around. There is no way I am going under by myself. When Thomas is right next to me, he grabs my arm, and we both turn around to see Lily and Nicole directly behind us.

"Can we all go under at the same time?" Thomas inquires.

"Okay," I say. "But we all need to be holding onto each other, because I don't trust you, guys. You are going to push me in or just not go or something."

Nicole laughs at this, probably knowing that, that is exactly what she was planning on doing. Thomas and I stand still waiting for Lily and Nicole to get next to us. Lily grabs onto Thomas's arm with Nicole on the opposite end as me.

"Okay, when I count to three, we are all going to step forward and go under," I say.

I wait for their consent and begin counting, "One...two..."

"No! Wait! I'm not ready yet," Nicole yells out, laughing like a hyena and clawing her way up Lily's arm.

"I'm scared! This water is so freaking cold!" she yells out again.

"C'mon, Nicole," Thomas grunts, annoyed at his sister.

"Okay, okay. I promise I will go in this time. You, guys, promise that you are going to go in too?" she asks.

We finally convince her that we are indeed going to go in. Thomas, annoyed at his sister prolonging the pain, takes the lead and warns us that he is going to count.

"Okay, you, guys, ready? One, two, three!"

Clinging to each other, we all take the three or so steps required to both reach the waterfall and step through its icy embrace, exiting its stream, and reaching our destination inside of the cave on the other side.

We are all yelling and cursing and jumping up and down inside of the cave, our heads numb from the pounding water on our heads. After a minute or so, we quiet down and realize that we have forgotten the shampoo. It is staring at us with a wicked smile from a rock on the other side of this frozen hell. At this point, I am amped up with so much adrenaline, I just run back through, grab the bottle, and run back into where everyone is waiting. Because I went and got it, I squeeze a glob onto my hand and hand the bottle to whoever's hand is reaching out for it. I massage it into my scalp, and without letting the anticipation of having to go back underneath the freezing water get the best of me, I run back under and quickly pump my hands through my hair so that the bubbles are all out. I then grab a bar of soap, run it all over my body and under my bathing suit, quickly rinse off, and then rapidly trek back to my towel, which is warmly calling my name from atop of the rock. Once I have my towel wrapped around me, I hear Nicole complaining that I should have waited for her. I inform her that I just had to get it over with. She is satisfied with this response, since she still has two partners waiting with her.

I sit on the edge of another rock, one where the sun has managed to sneak through the trees just enough to blanket. It feels extra inviting after that freezing waterfall shower. Although it was deathly cold during the time, I honestly don't think I have ever felt more clean or refreshed. I tip my head back and feel the sun on my face. I can hear the chatter of my friends in the background, but I'm not really paying attention to what they are saying.

I know that adults sometimes talk about how being a teenager is hard. I sometimes feel like that too. Like, life has to be easier someday. I hate meeting new people when my friends aren't around. I also hate how my mom doesn't seem to understand my feelings a majority of the time. I often feel like I am floating around in the world, with all of these people around me going about their daily lives, and none of them understand me and who I am. I also feel like none of them will ever love me the way my friends do. This thought is often too much for me to deal with. But right now, I am so happy, and I feel like I don't need anyone else in the world to understand me as long as I have my friends.

I am taken out of my thoughts as the volume of my friends' chatter grows in intensity. They are right next to me now, wrapping themselves in towels and making their way over to my prized rock. They each find a spot surrounding me and my rock and sit, knowing what comes next. Thomas opens his backpack and hands us each a cigarette. Thomas lights his first, then passes the lighter to Lily, who hands it to Nicole, who hands it to me. The first drag feels like life being blown back into me. My icy lungs have suddenly warmed.

After we have finished our cigarettes in near silence, Thomas informs us that we need to head back to the campground. He said that he thinks that we are going to some big lake or something today, and if we are gone too long, his dad will be mad. We all run our hands back through the icy water to rid ourselves of the smell, pack up our stuff, and head back to the bicycles. Automatically, our previous handlebar passengers are now the riders. I hop up on top, a small smile spread across my face, and again tip my face up toward the sun, thanking Mother Nature for this splendid day to spend in the company of my other quarters.

A few hours and an hour-napped car ride later, we arrive at what looks like a giant lake. We all sleepily exit the car and follow

Mr. Rosetti and his friend Walter down a grassy path that leads to the bank of the lake.

"What are we supposed to do here, Dad?" Nicole inquires.

"We are going to take turns going out on the canoe. You guys can swim. Figure it out."

Nicole unfolds her towel, spreads it out on a giant flat rock, and lays down immediately closing her eyes. We all follow her lead and lay our towels down beside hers. I, Lily, and Thomas sit up, our eyes drawn to the seemingly local teenagers, who are taking turns jumping off of this old bridge that runs over the middle of the lake. As Nicole sleeps peacefully next to us, we quietly watch these kids lift one leg, then the other, and carefully climb over the barrier on the roadside of the bridge, until they are on the other side of the barrier, looking down at the water below. I am not sure about Lily or Thomas, but this is one of those moments where I am getting sweaty palms and that topsy-turvy feeling in my stomach just watching these kids climb over, get the guts, and finally jump, legs and arms grasping for something that isn't there in the air before loudly splashing into the water below. I am not afraid of heights, but this seems scary to me.

Mr. Rosetti suddenly yells over to us, "Do you guys want to jump?"

I look over at Thomas and Lily, who both don't say anything, but look at me with frightened expressions.

"Jess, c'mon. You aren't afraid are you? The others need you to do it first, and then they will too," Mr. Rossetti adds.

Although this seems like peer pressure, I know that Mr. Rosetti is right. He has known me my entire life, and what seems like him pressuring me into doing something, I know is just him treating me like the bravest of one of his own kids. I look over at Thomas and Lily.

Thomas says, "If you do it, I will too."

I think about this for a moment. I mean, I love doing adventurous things. I am so incredibly scared, not that I want to admit this to anyone. Being brave is part of who I am. But if those other kids are doing it and they are fine, I will be fine too. I convince myself of this, before saying, "Okay, I will do it if everyone comes over with me."

"There you go, Jess. All right, guys, c'mon over," Mr. Rosetti presses.

I nudge Nicole, who has since woken up and is also staring at the kids jumping off of the bridge. I get up and shakily make my way over to the bridge, my friends all following behind.

When I get to the bridge, I look over at the group of kids just to my left. There are two girls in this group of six. The girls are not jumping. They are watching the boys taking turns making the plunge into this foggy greenish lake. For whatever reason, the fact that they are not jumping makes me want to jump even more. Acting like one of the guys has always been my go-to way of trying to impress guys. However, it usually winds up with them being my friend and confiding in me about the girl that they like, usually Lily. Anyway, I feel like I need to just do it and do it fast before I change my mind or anyone notices how nervous I really am. I steal a quick glance at Lily, who looks so nervous and is clinging to both Thomas and Nicole's arm. If I thought that my friends were going to help encourage me, I was wrong. They all look so scared and like they aren't quite sure what to say.

I look at Mr. Rosetti, who still has a smile plastered to his face. "Well, are you going to go, Jess?"

"Yes. I am just trying to figure out where I should jump from."

He directs me to an open spot, just to the right of the other group of kids, and says, "The water is a bit darker over here. It's probably the deepest spot."

"Okay," I say and follow him over to the suggested spot.

I am happy when I feel him grab my arms while I slip my first leg over. It is nice to know that he is looking out for me and that I am not completely and utterly alone over here. I quickly slide my other leg over, grasping onto Mr. Rosetti's forearms for support. My hands are so clammy. I wonder how I am even going to hold onto the barrier. Mr. Rosetti gives me a second to wipe my hands off on the front of my bathing suit before letting go of me. As soon as he lets go of me, I turn around and face the foggy green lake—she seems to be eagerly anticipating chomping me up in one bite.

"Okay. I'm going to count to three, and then go. Are you, guys, ready?" My voice is suddenly shaky, and any nervousness that I was trying to conceal is completely obvious. Before I can even change my mind, I quickly count, "One, two, three!" and I jump.

My stomach instantly lurches through my being. I plaster my arms to my side and head for the murky lake. Before I can even think about how scared I am, I gulp my last bit of air before plunging in. I am going down and down, and then I feel my feet touch the soft muddy bottom of the lake. I push off of the bottom with all of my strength, and I push my arms up to fight for the surface as fast as I can. My head emerges, and I take the most satisfying breath of my lifetime. I look up to the bridge and see the faces of my three best friends smiling at me, and I hear them cheering my name. I smile back. I hear Thomas yell down, "How was it, Jess?"

And I, of course, have to admit that now that I am alive, "It was so fun!" I swim slowly but excitedly to the bank where I can climb out and walk back up to the bridge.

I don't quite understand why I always feel the need to be the first one to do this crazy stuff. Maybe there isn't enough craziness in my life to compete with my friends, so I have to make up for it somehow. I always seem to be chasing this ever-present need for adventure in one way or another, but I must admit—that was utterly amazing.

Now that I have done it, everyone else has got to give it a try. Mr. Rosetti and Walter are even taking a brief pause from their canoe plans to join us in our jumping endeavors. Thomas, Lily, and Nicole all want to jump at the same time, and I tell them that I will come too. We argue about who will hold whose hand and stand next to whom for a few minutes before we agree on me in the middle with Nicole on one side, Lily on the other, and Thomas on Lily's end. I scramble back over the ledge first. The only wetness on my hands this time is the remaining lake water that is still dripping down my body from my head. When we all make it over, we squish next to each other, grab each other's arms, count to three, and jump. The excitement is still there for me this time; however, it's more of a comfortable excitement. I am having so much fun, and this time I am with my three best friends, so whatever happens, I'm not alone. And that is enough for me to smile my biggest possible smile. Our bodies race toward the lake. We all let go of each other at the last second and hit the water, our bodies disappearing beneath its muddy green body. I feel the bottom of the lake again and push off of it as quickly as possible. I am eager to get to the surface, more to gauge the reactions of my friends than to get that breath of fresh air.

We spent the day jumping off of that bridge, God knows how many times. We swam through that lake, jumping and pulling on each other in the shallow water as our feet stepped on all sorts of unknown lake grasses and creatures. We lay in the sun, talking of what life would be like if we could live here forever. We all took turns with Mr. Rosetti in the canoe, which turned out to actually be a lot of fun. We snuck off to smoke cigarettes, using our bladders as excuses to go hide in the woods. We napped in the sun, in the shade, and now everyone but me is napping in the van on the way back to the campground. Stevie Nicks and Don Henly's "Leather and Lace" quietly plays in the background. My eyes are closed, but I haven't yet drifted off to sleep. Happiness is hard to describe. Is it the actual act of laughing? Is it the lack of crying? Is it just being?

Chapter 11

BOAT DAY

There is one week left until summer officially begins. Between that and the fact that Thomas and Nicole agreed to go out on their boat today, I am feeling quite happy. Boat days are my favorite. Thomas and Nicole aren't fazed by it—actually they often need to be persuaded to go. However, for me, it's pure joy. When we were little, their dad didn't have to do much to coax them into going, but as they've gotten older, I guess there are other things they'd rather be doing. All of that aside, today I talk them into going by claiming it a late birthday gift. Despite all of their complaining, they always end up having fun.

At 7:00 AM, I sleepily walk across the street; my flip flops are the only sound present in the neighborhood. As I walk through Thomas and Nicole's front door, I hear their dad, "Nicole, get your ass up, we're leavin' in seven minutes."

I then hear Nicole's yelling from her room, her raspy sleepy sweetness clouding the morning, "Then leave without me, I don't wanna go anyway!"

"Try me, Nicole, if you're not in the van in seven minutes, your ass is grass. Hi, Jess, will you get Tom and Nicole out of their beds." This was not a question.

I walk down the hallway and walk into Thomas's room first. He is crawling out of bed as I walk through the door. Lily is perched on the side of his bed. "Hey, Jess" she replies.

"Hey, Lil, where did you get those shorts?"

Lily is wearing these amazing board shorts.

"Oh, my grandma took me shopping yesterday for babysitting Kit and James."

"Oh, they're awesome."

"Thanks."

Just at this moment, Nicole walks through the door mumbling how she hates her father and how he is an asshole. "Lily, why didn't you wake me up?"

"I tried to like ten times. You scare the shit out of me when you're sleeping. I didn't want you to try to strangle me again."

"You are being dramatic. I told you I won't do that again unless she makes me. The only reason I did that last time was because the witch came inside and told me to."

Nicole sometimes acts like a maniac. She chokes Lily and me, laughs creepily, chases us with knives through the house, and then just blames it on the "witch" that is inside of her. I don't know where she gets this from, but it's so scary. I don't think she would actually hurt any of us, but I think we are all a little bit scared of Nicole.

Soon after Nicole wakes up, we all go get in the van; and without any words, go straight to our usual spots. Nicole goes immediately to the second row and lays across the whole seat. Thomas, Lily, and I go to the last row, knees resting against the back of the second row, heads dipped low into our seats. We close our eyes and take a short seven-minute nap to the marina.

When we arrive at the dock, we hop out of the van and drowsily walk over to sit on the curb while Mr. Rosetti carefully angles the truck in order to perfectly reverse the boat into its slot. I'm not sure if it's the gloriously disgusting smell of low tide, but our energy is beginning to increase. We have gotten through the hard part, waking up and actually getting here. Everyone is finally realizing that we are going to have fun.

After Mr. Rosetti and his dive buddy Bill are done setting up, they anchor the boat and grab our arms as they guide us onto the boat. As soon as I step on, that comforting sway fills my insides with peace. We, kids, walk to the front of the boat and sit in a curved row around the bow. From as far back as I can remember, these have been our spots. Even as little kids, Thomas, Nicole, and I loved to sit up here and feel the bumps as the boat flew across the waves. Every third bump was the big one, the salty ocean spray slamming us in our squinty sun-scorched eyes and Silly Putty smiles. Our impermeable laughter was infectious and contagious. This is one of the reasons I love going on the boat; it's one of the only places on earth that I still feel like a little kid. It's during these moments when we fly across the waves that my laughter and enjoyment make it impossible to think of anything but the present joy I'm experiencing.

Today is no different. As soon as we pass the slow point, the boat speeds up. Our "Black Hole Sun" smiles immediately stretch across our faces, and I look at my friends and know that they are just as happy as I am.

In about a half an hour, after numerous bumps and laughs, we finally arrive at a little isolated island. We anchor the boat in shallow water, climb down the steps at the back of the boat, try not to breathe in motor gas fumes, and walk slowly, towels held high above our heads to the island. As soon as we get there, we lay our towels next to each other and lie down. After a few unimportant words, our talk dies down, and we close our eyes and soak up the summer's smile. I can hear the sound of Mr. Rosetti and Bill putting on their dive gear, checking each other's stuff, and then their voices as they walk backward into the water, "Bye, guys, we'll be back in a few hours."

As soon as their heads disappear from view, Nicole sneakily pulls a cigarette out of I don't know where and lights it up. It is one of her mom's Marlboro Light 100's.

"Can I have a drag, Nic?" She leans over Thomas and Lily and puts the cigarette to my lips.

I pull deeply, and am feeling happy. I love the sound of the waves lapping against the shore and my best friends' bodies next to me.

"Let's explore!" came Nicole's voice out of nowhere. She is already up and walking toward the grassy dunes.

"Wait up. I'm coming," I quickly say as I get up and run to catch up to her.

"Come on, Thomas and Lily," I say.

"I'm staying. I don't feel like getting up right now. Where are you going, Nicole?" Thomas yells.

"I don't know. I'm just walking."

"Give me one of mom's cigarettes."

"I don't have anymore."

"Liar."

Lily and Thomas stay behind. *Ughhhhh.* Sibling banter. "Wait, Nicole I'm coming. You are walking too fast."

"All right, Billy," Nicole says and hooks my arm with hers.

We walk around the perimeter of the small island with our arms sweatily interlaced. When Nicole has found the spot that she has been searching for, she plops down on a small wall of sand and starts digging in her shorts. I am confused for a second until I realize that she is pulling out a bowl and some weed.

"What! You really want to smoke that right now? Aren't you afraid of your dad knowing you are stoned?"

"No, they just left. They won't be back for a few hours."

I think about this for a second, and am kind of nervous about the possibility of Mr. Rosetti discovering that we are stoned, but my excitement outweighs my fear. A few seconds later, she digs under her boobs and pulls out a lighter, one of Leann's Bic. She smokes first, and then passes it to me. I pull long and hard and immediately smile. After a good ten minutes of silent coughing and passing, we are done.

We look at each other and laugh. I stand up and do a roll in the sand and stop flat on my back. Nicole comes and jumps on me laughing. We stand up and continue our stroll around the island. This time we walk with our feet through the shallow water and kicking up sprays of water. I begin singing "A Day in the Life" as I walk and kick and smile my squinty, stoned smile at the day.

Nicole breaks my stoned nonsense with, "I feel like I don't fit in anywhere."

I shockingly reply, "What do you mean? We have been best friends since we were born."

"It's just different. You and Thomas and Lily are different. You have all of these separate friends, and you, guys, hang out without me all of the time. It's not like it used to be, and I miss you."

I am in utter shock. I quickly reply, "Nicole, what are you talking about. We still hang out all of the time. You have other friends that you hang out with without us."

"Yea, but, the three of you are always together. When I hang out without you, guys, I am by myself. You, guys, are always together."

I am silent for a moment before I reply this time. I have never really thought too much about this. I just assume it was a natural progression. I never really thought about what it was like for her. I just thought that she wanted to create some space between her and Thomas. I thought that there was mutual understanding between all of us.

"I think that sometimes things change when you get older. I mean, we sometimes hang out with different people, but we are like sisters. We will always be best friends."

She doesn't say anything for a few seconds. She must be satisfied with my assessment of the situation, because she soon just says, "Okay," and we continue walking.

I don't know about Nicole, but I am having one of those moments where you kind of get lost in time. I feel like I wasn't exactly thinking about anything, but we just kept walking, and then the next thing I know, Thomas and Lily are in our view. They are sitting across from each other, Thomas's back is to us, and I can tell even from far away that Lily is either crying or sad based on the way that she is holding her knees with her head drooping toward them. I look over at Nicole and ask, "Is Lily crying?"

She looks in their direction, then back at me and says, "Probably," and leaves it at that.

Lily must notice us approaching, because she wipes her cheeks and smiles at us, indicating that whatever she was crying about is over and done with and that she no longer wants to talk about it. I'm sure that she and Thomas were just rehashing old issues. She does this to herself all of the time. She loves Thomas with every fiber of her being, and she knows that he is gay. But there is this part of her that thinks that if they were together once, maybe he can feel the same way about her again. According to my mom, he was her first love, and there will always be a part or her that will be sad when thinking about the fact that they are no longer together. I know that Lily understands that they will never be together again, but it's almost as if she keeps dwelling on their relationship so much that she isn't leaving room to ever feel anything for anyone else.

I plop down on Lily's towel and smash myself really close to her to let her know that I love her. Thankfully Thomas looks at Nicole and breaks the awkwardness by saying, "Are you, guys, stoned?"

I look at Nicole and we both start laughing.

"What the hell, guys. You went and smoked without us. That is so messed up."

Nicole defends herself by saying, "You didn't want to come with us."

"I would have come if I knew that you were going to smoke. Where did you even get weed from?"

"Sorry, brother man, you snooze, you lose."

I'm not sure if it is because I am high, but I laugh so hard when she says this. She sounds like a tiny version of her mom. Leanne has a million of these weird old people sayings that are just like that. You will often hear Nicole shout things like, "Your ass is grass!" or "Not for nothing," when we are all out in public places. She knows that the rest of us think these sayings are awful, so she does it purposely in order to obtain a reaction from us. Actually, in this case, she utilized it perfectly, because both Lily and Thomas are now laughing with me. I decide to roll back on my elbows and do my Peter Pan pose. As soon as I fling myself back, my legs flying in the air, I am overcome with a bout of the giggles. I start laughing and can't stop. After only a few seconds, I am laughing so hard that I am weak and just let myself fall over. I start rolling through the sand toward the water, laughing like a crazed person. My laughter is contagious. Thomas, Lily, and Nicole chase after me laughing and jump on top of me when I get to the water's edge. All four of us are rolling around in the water laughing at nothing. We are sacks of bodies weak with laughter. It only takes a few minutes for all of our energy to be gone. Everyone else has stopped laughing. They are all looking at me, almost waiting for me to entertain them with more of my irrational conduct.

I pull myself together and stand up. "Whew. Well, now that, that's over, I'm going to go lay in, in the sun," I manage to say without breaking into more reasonless cackling.

I steadily walk back to my towel and drop down and create a little pillow with my folded arms out in front of me. I hear my friends lying beside me. The presence of their bodies lying next to me informs my body that it can let go for a short while.

None of us wake up until we hear Mr. Rosetti's thundering voice informing us that it's time to leave. I can hear him, but it sounds so far away. It's like my body wants to lift my head up, but I am trapped inside this sleepy world. I give myself another minute, and then am able to open my eyes and lift my head up. I look over and see that my friends are in the exact same "I have no idea how long we have been sleeping" stage. I think about how when we were kids, sleeping on one of these trips would be the last thing we would ever want to do; as a kid, you don't want to chance missing out on anything. As children, Thomas, Nicole, and I would spend hours just running around and exploring on one of these islands; and now we have wasted a good portion of the afternoon napping. This is actually not typical behavior for me at all. My friends all stay up late; hence, they love taking naps in the middle of the day. But me, I am going to just blame the pot.

We drowsily grab our towels, slip our shoes on, and make our way toward the boat. Once we are on, without asking, Mr. Rosetti hands us each an apple and a sandwich that Leanne packed for us this morning. I didn't realize how hungry I was until I took my first bite of the sandwich. We all quietly sit on the floor on the back of the boat and scarf down the food. When we are done, we each take a swig of Thomas's water bottle, then head back to the bow and claim our standard spots.

The trip home is very serene. We are all pretty quiet at first. But as soon as we hit the open ocean and the boat picks up speed, we all smile again. The spray is hitting our faces and washing off the quiet lethargy of our afternoon naps. I feel refreshed. I'm not sure what time it is, but the sun is getting low in the sky and creating those beautiful sparkles on the tips of each wave. I feel like I can go home and tell my mom all about my day, minus the smoking cigarettes and pot part. I want to tell her about how much fun it was exploring the island, about how we spent a majority of the day laughing, and lastly how beautiful the world looks at this exact moment. I realize how perfect today has been, and I don't think that even if I could muster up some truly awesome visuals to describe some of the things that I saw today. I don't think that I could ever really describe the things I'm feeling right now. I could try by saying, "I feel completely at ease," like my body is so utterly relaxed and my breathing feels easier than easy. I feel such a sense of contentment, like there is nowhere else I could even imagine being. I feel like no one anywhere on earth could possibly be more at peace than I am right now, sitting next to my best friends, on a boat, with the sun setting, and seeing that rainbow of diamonds dance across the waves. It is just so sublime, and the words that I am using and the way in which I am using them could never describe it accurately enough, so I guess I'll just say it was a superb day, and leave it at that.

Chapter 12

GIRLS' NIGHT

"Girls' Night" is one of my all-time favorite weekend activities. Nicole and I, with her mom acting as organizer, have been enjoying these adventures since we were little girls. However, the activities have changed somewhat throughout the years. Whenever Thomas and Mr. Rosetti plan some kind of weekend upstate "boys only" camping adventure, Leanne immediately calls my mom and asks her if I can sleep over. As little girls, Nicole and I would pull out the couch bed in the living room and watch cheesy movies like *The Mask* with Jim Carey and eat popcorn and dance around the living room. Now that we are older, we have traded the movie with music and the popcorn with cigs and sometimes beer. These days, Lily always joins us, and we spend the night blasting oldies out of the Bose stereo, dancing around in our pajamas and singing along at the tops of our lungs. We eat and laugh and sweat until we all pass out in the same bed, arms and legs intertwined. It has been at least six months since we've had a "girls' night." I am so excited that we finally get to have one tonight. I just need to throw on my pajamas and head over there.

It takes me six seconds to walk from my house across the street. As I walk up the narrow sidewalk, I can hear "Mr. Postman" blaring through the giant double front window. I walk through the front door and see Lily and Nicole swinging through the chorus, elbows locked, teenage giggles surrounding them. Leanne walks from the kitchen, a cigarette in one hand, a can in the other. I automatically hold my fake microphone to my lips and let out the tail end of the song; the song drifts out and the room echoes with heavy breathing and giggles.

"Hey, guys, how long have you been dancing?" I get out, just as "Leader of the Pack" comes on.

"Just a few minutes," Lily and Nicole both say, each a fraction of a second after the other, so that their voices create a cheerful melody.

"My mom got us forties," Nicole belts out.

I hear Leanne yell from the kitchen, "Jess, don't tell ya motha, or she won't let ya sleep ova here anymore."

I want to say that my mother already doesn't want me to sleep over here and that there is no way I would tell her that. If my mom even thought for a second that banning me from the company of my best friends was any use, she would have attempted it ages ago. Although my mom does not trust Leanne in the slightest, I know that she has no idea that she sometimes buys us alcohol.

"We waited for you, Jess," Lily responds excitedly.

"Thanks, guys," I say, and I am genuinely thankful.

Leanne walks out of the kitchen clutching all three forty ounces and waits as we each walk up to her, give her a thank-you kiss, and ceremoniously receive our gift. Nicole and Lily go first. When it's my turn, Leanne also makes me tell her that I love her before she will hand me the goods. She has been doing it for years. She then tells Lily, "You know I love ya too, Lil, but I changed this one's diapez."

After finally getting my beverage, all of us open our tops, click our jugs, and take in about ten solid seconds of first sip glory. As soon as I taste the bubbles, I know tonight will be just as fun as I anticipated.

"Duke of Earl" blares wildly as Nicole, Lily, and I form our familiar dance circle. We dip low with every "duke, duke, duke," until we are sitting on the floor right next to the speaker, still in our circle.

Nicole's voice yells, "On the count of three, chug! One, two, three!"

We all tip our forties and chug until the bubbles and burn are too much.

After a few more songs, Leanne saunters in, walks around our circle as she shakes her boobs in each of our faces. She then leans over Nicole and places her cigarette in Nicole's mouth from behind.

"What about me?" Lily chimes in.

Leanne brings the cigarette to Lily's lips as she runs her hands through Lily's beautiful dark silky mane. Next, Leanne walks behind me and gives me a drag. I am starting to feel glorious.

Within the hour, we are down to the ass of our forties. Even though I think it all must be backwash, all of us finish them. I look over at Lily and realize that she has ripped the label off of her bottle. The two of us have a habit of peeling while we drink.

Leanne glides into the room as Nicole sits on my lap and sways to "Teenager in Love." Leanne squeezes past us and turns the volume even louder and slurs at us, "Get the hell up and dans with me."

This would normally have turned into an argument between Nicole and her mom, but she, like the rest of us, is feeling too good to resist. We all get up, lean into each other, and sing, "Each night I ask, the stars up above / Why must I be a teenager in love?"

I think that this song is beautiful, but it is just too much for Lily to handle right now. I see her eyes getting red, and then the tears come. We are all used to this. We don't even have to ask Lily why she is crying. Leanne knows too.

She chimes in, "I know his my son, but screw 'em."

Leanne tosses her hands into the air. Pauses for a second and starts again, "He loves you so mich…look at me." She grabs Lily by the chin and forces her to look at her face. "He loves you, Lil…He's jus…not that way."

Lily doesn't say anything and neither do Nicole nor me. We all know that Thomas loves Lily, but it's just not in the way that she wants him to love her.

I try to shed some light, "Lily, there are a million boys at school who would love to go out with you. You are so pretty and smart and cool. I see people checking you out all of the time. You need to move on. Thomas does love you. So do Nicole and I. We are all best friends. Thomas will always love you as a best friend."

"I'm sorry, guys. I told myself I wasn't going to do this tonight. I'm done now. I'm okay," Lily says as a small fake smile breaks through.

"Mom, can we have a cigarette for Lily?" Nicole yells to her mom who has walked back to the kitchen.

"Tell her to come heah and git it," Leanne slurs.

Lily gets up, wipes the tears from her face on her Nightmare Before Christmas pajama pants. Right when Lily gets up, Nicole puts her face right next to my ear and whispers, "My mother is so drunk. How the hell did she get like that? I don't think she could have had a lot more than us. It's only been like an hour."

I don't respond. I'm thinking about what she just said, but I don't want to be the person to tell her that her mom looks more than just drunk.

"I don't know, Nicole. But let's sneak into her room and grab a cigarette while she is talking to Lily."

"Good idea," she replies.

Nicole gets up and gets on all fours and starts to seductively crawl across the floor while twisting her face into these hideous grins. She crawls backward and purposely sticks her ass in my face until I fall backward. I slap her ass as hard as I can while giggling wildly. She yells, "Ow, you, bitch!" and crawls away. I watch as she slithers past the kitchen entrance and continues on toward her parents' bedroom. I am left with my thoughts. I am warm and fuzzy and at peace. My eyes are a bit heavy and my smile permanent.

I look up and see Nicole walking back from the bedroom all nonchalantly as if she had just went to the bathroom. When she passes the kitchen, she picks up the pace, giggles in her witchy way, and jumps on my lap, sitting facing me and plants a huge kiss right on my forehead.

"Did you get one?" I whisper.

She glances over her shoulder, sees that her mom is not coming back, and pulls two Marlboro 100's from in between her boobs. She replaces them, grabs my hand, pulls me up, and we automatically start our slow-dancing routine. Our fingers of one hand are clasped so that we can pump our locked arms in and out as it leads the direction from one side of the room to the other. We know that "Crimson and Clover" is not really a "slow song," but we always do this dance no matter what is on. Nicole keeps changing directions before I'm ready, which causes me to jerk all over the living room. We are both laughing so wildly, and Nicole won't stop pulling me in every which direction that we suddenly fall to the floor in a laughing heap of ridiculousness. Nicole's witchy wild laugh is so loud, and she's purposely making this scrunchie face that makes her laugh all nasally and crazy sounding. It is so ridiculous that I start to laugh even louder. I scrunch up my face, and we both laugh so loud and nasally and obnoxiously. We are rolling around the living room, a nasally laughing mess. Lily steps out of the kitchen smiling.

"What the hell are you guys doing?" Lily says with a grin.

She runs over and jumps on us and starts laughing with us until all of our lungs are aching.

* * *

About an hour later, we are sitting on the back deck. It is a beautiful night. We don't even need hoodies. I can feel the summer approaching, and it makes me even more happy. Lily and I are sitting with our legs resting on the bars under the table, while Nicole has her legs resting on mine. We are passing around one of the stolen cigarettes. Leanne is passed out in her room. We each take an allotted two drags and pass it on. Nicole is first to break the silence, "I love you, bitches. You guys are like my sistas."

"Love you too, Biff," I reply using my childhood nickname for her.

"Love you too," Lily adds.

"No, I like really love you, guys. You are my like my family. Do you promise that we'll stay friends forever?"

"Of course, we will. Why wouldn't we?" I say.

"I don't know. I'm just making sure."

Lily says, "Of course, we will. That's a stupid question, Biffy."

"Well, I'm tired. Let's go to bed."

Lily and I stand up and follow Nicole. We all drop into bed and squirm into our usual spots. I can tell that Nicole and Lily are asleep within minutes by the sound of their breathing. I try hard not to let my mind wander so that I can fall asleep faster. When I can tell that that tactic is not going to work, I give up and start thinking about my day. I had so much fun, felt warm and happy, so much fun laughing, rolling on the floor, talking, and friends.

Chapter 13

PAT'S HOUSE

It's finally summer! Yesterday was our last day of school. I was able to turn around all of my grades for the fourth quarter, and I managed to pass all of my classes! Woo hoo! I thought I would have to go to summer school, but I somehow managed to get through. I think it was all of that time I was grounded and was trapped in my room. I had nothing else to do so I did my homework instead. I also tried to think of how terrible my summer would be if I was trapped in my room all day, while my friends were hanging out all day. This is our last summer of freedom. Next summer, we will all have to get jobs.

Today Pat invited us over to go swimming in his pool. I am excited to see him, but I am so nervous about being in my bathing suit in front of him. I am not shy at all in front of my closest friends, but I always feel like Pat is checking me out. And I can't even look at him, and my cheeks get all blushy, and it's just so embarrassing. I also know that he is going to try to kiss me today. We have been talking on the phone a lot, and he tells me how much he likes me. I really like him too, but I am really nervous about having a boyfriend. He has asked me a million times to please go out with him, but I just keep saying no. It really isn't that I don't want to. I am just so scared. I know that Pat has had sex before, and I just can't even imagine saying

I don't want to or be put in that situation. I know that when Thomas and Lily were together, they had sex all the time. Nicole has had sex with two boyfriends of hers. I am the only one who hasn't had sex. I know that I am in high school, and I shouldn't be nervous about kissing him. But it has been forever since I have kissed someone. Thomas and I kissed when we were kids, but it wasn't intimate. We used mouthwash first and kissed in my room when I had babysitters and pretended to play board games. That was years ago. I have never kissed anyone that I really liked.

So anyway, my mom agreed to drive us all over to Pat's. My mom likes his mother and also likes the idea that we are going to be "swimming in the pool" all day. I guess swimming in the pool seems innocent to her or something. Anyway, I'm borrowing Lily's two-piece bathing suit, because we are basically the same size. I stare at myself in the mirror and hate what I see. Lily is perfectly slender with skinny arms and legs and a flat stomach. I have muscles everywhere, and I feel like I look like a man. I have big shoulders, arms, and thigh muscles and muscles bulging out of my stomach. I used to be a gymnast, and my body just won't ever look normal again. My mom always tells me I look "healthy" and "athletic," but that doesn't make me feel any better. I'm not stupid. I know that boys like Lily not only because she is pretty, but because she has the most amazing body. No one ever says, "Wow, Jess is hot. She looks like a bodybuilder."

"C'mon, Jess, are you ready?" my mom yells as she sticks her head into my room.

"Where did you get that bathing suit?"

"Oh hi, Mom! It's Lily's, she's letting me borrow it."

"What's wrong with your bathing suit? Do you not like it any-more?" I always feel terrible when she asks me things like this. I feel like I am disappointing her because I am not wearing the new bathing suit she got me.

"No, I like it, Mom. It's just in the wash."

"Oh, okay. I will make sure I wash it before this weekend. I was hoping that we could all go to the beach on Sunday and have breakfast like we used to when you and Matt were little."

"Yea, that sounds great, Ma."

"Okay, well c'mon. I have errands to run after I drop ya off. Are Nicole and Thomas going to be ready?"

"Yea, Ma, I called them like a half hour ago and reminded them."

"All right, well let's go."

I sit in the passenger seat and take charge of the radio. I immediately put on K-Rock. This is fine with my mom as long as it isn't too loud. In two seconds, we are across the street beeping outside of the Rosetti's. Within seconds, Thomas, Nicole, and Lily are walking out. Nicole and Lily have boxers over their bathing suits with just their tops showing. Thomas has the Scott Weiland shirt he made over his bathing suit. I have a T-shirt on top of my boxers as well. I don't think I can deal with showing up in just my bathing suit without a T-shirt over it. They all plop in the back seat and say hi to my mom.

"Hi, guys," she replies.

"Does your mom know you're going ova to Pat's?"

"Yea, I woke her up this morning and told her. Who knows if she will remember later?" Nicole replies.

No one replies to this; we know what she means. We blast down the highway the seven minutes it takes us to get to Pat's house. The air is warm, and the radio is blaring. My mom reaches over and tells me to "turn off that garbage" when Rammstein comes on. She switches the station with her free hand and turns on John Cougar Mellancamp's "Wild Night." This is such a mom song, but we all loved it when we were little. So we all sing along, nice and loud so my mom knows that changing the station isn't going to make things any quieter. When we get to Pat's, I give my mom a kiss and tell her I will call her later when I know whether or not I need a ride home. She smells like summer and my mom and comfort. I get even more nervous about kissing Pat. There is a part of me that wants to hop back in the car and go home and sit in the backyard on a blanket while my mom gardens like I used to when I was little.

As we walk up Pat's driveway, we see that he has heard us arrive. He walks out of the side door and tells us to come in the backyard. He has a boom box with him to put some music on.

"Is your mom home?" Thomas asks Pat.

"No, she is at work until 1:00 PM. She will be home later."

"Can we smoke a cigarette in your backyard?" Thomas asks.

"Yea, lemme go get a cup with some water in it to put your ashes and butts in."

Pat gets up to go get the cup, and Thomas leans toward me as we all squeeze on one of the benches, "Jess, are you going to kiss Pat today?"

"Ughh. Why does everyone keep asking me that? I don't know. I guess we'll see."

"Well, do you like him?" Thomas asks in his curious whisper.

"Well, yea, but I don't know if I want a boyfriend."

"Why not? You are so weird, Jess. Are you sure you aren't a lesbo?"

"Shut up, Thomas. You know how mad that makes me."

"Okay, sorry, Jess. But why won't you go out with him. He's cute."

"Shhhhh!" I say, as he walks back outside.

Pat puts on The Beatles "Rubber Soul," which instantly makes me happy. After two cigarettes, countless sing-a-longs, and Pat telling us stories about our other friends we haven't seen yet this summer, Pat asks us if we want to go in the pool. I honestly don't want to be in a bathing suit right now, but everyone else says they want to go in. Everyone starts taking off T-shirts and boxers and making their way to the pool. I quickly take off my boxers and T-shirt when I think that no one's looking and immediately pull my towel around me. I try to look natural and like I am not shy. I walk with my towel around me all the way up the deck stairs to the pool, wait until everyone else is in, and have their heads turned to throw my towel over the banister and jump in. Once I am in the water and feel like my body is covered, I feel better again. We all swim around and pull each other's legs so that our faces end up in the water. I try to stay away from Pat so that I can act like myself. After a few minutes, I hear Pat's voice behind me, "Hey, Jess, can you come talk to me for a second?"

"Yea, sure." I immediately feel my heart pounding. I am so nervous. I can barely look at him.

I hate that our friendship has changed since he admitted that he likes me. We used to just flirt and have fun all the time. I hate that things have changed. I am trying so hard to act natural and like I am not nervous. I follow Pat over to the other side of the pool.

"Jess, why are you ignoring me?"

"I'm not ignoring you" I say.

"I'm just hanging out with everyone."

Pat replies, "You are acting so weird around me. You were perfectly fine last night when we were talking on the phone."

"I know. I'm sorry. I didn't think I was ignoring you."

I peek over my shoulder because it just got quiet. I see Nicole look at me and smile and say, "I'm getting cold. I am gonna get out and go sit in the sun."

"Me too," both Lily and Thomas say, looking a little too happy.

I know that they are trying to leave Pat and me alone. I feel set up.

"Well, anyway," Pat says. "Please be my girlfriend, Jess. I really, really like you. Please. Please. Please," looking at me with the most desperate face.

I mean, I want to have a boyfriend. I am just scared. I know that if I were ever to have a boyfriend, it should be Pat.

"Okay," I say and give him a nervous smile.

"Finally!" he says, and he really does look happy.

He leans in and gives me a huge hug. He squeezes me so tight that he lifts my feet off of the bottom of the pool. Within moments, I see it. There it is. That look. I know he is going to want to kiss me. My heart is jumping. There is a part of me that really wants to, that wishes that I wasn't such a wuss. I wish I was normal like all of my friends and didn't put so much thought into this. Everyone else just does it, just kisses people all of the time. It is not that big a deal.

Pat is looking at me with that sweet, nervous face and says, "Jess, can I kiss you?"

I can't say no. I just agreed to be his girlfriend. He looks so happy.

"Yea," I say.

That is all I can muster. Pat grabs my face gently, his hands wrapped almost around my head, and pulls me in. He starts by giving me a sweet peck on the lips. I am surprised by how natural it feels to kiss him. I look up at him, smile, and then lean back in for a real kiss. Within moments, I realize that we are a perfect kissing pair. This kiss is utterly magical; it is slow and sweet and exciting and perfect. After about a minute, I hug him as we continue to kiss. He hugs me back and pulls me in close. I am so happy.

After what has probably been at least fifteen minutes of kissing, I am actually really starting to get cold. Pat can feel me shivering and asks if I want to get out.

"Yea, okay," I say.

I look up at him and he looks happy but nervous. I have to look away. I have no idea how it is so difficult to look someone in the eye who you just spent the last fifteen minutes making out with. Pat climbs out first, and then grabs my towel for me. He holds it out like my mom used to when I was little so that when I pull myself out, I can just climb into its warmth. He hugs me again while I am all wrapped in my towel. He looks so happy. His happiness makes me happy as well. I really want to grab my friends and get away from all of this and talk about the kiss, but I can't run away now. It will look way too weird.

"Hey, guys!" Nicole yells at us from over on the bench.

She has this huge smile on her face, and I know that all of them know exactly what is going on.

"Are you guys going out now?" she blurts out.

Nicole is like that, very brash; she says whatever is on her mind at the moment. That's what gets her into trouble all of the time at school. Pat looks over at me, still smiling and says, "Yea, we are."

"It's about freaking time," Nicole says.

"Shut up!" I say, but I am smiling and blushing at the same time.

"Do you, guys, want to share this last cigarette? We were waiting for you guys to get out of the pool. You were in there forever" Nicole continues.

"Thanks for waiting, guys," I say, and I mean it. I am so nervous that I really need a cigarette right now to calm down a bit.

After the four of us share the cigarette and have each chosen a CD from Pat's collection, his mom pulls up. She immediately comes to the backyard to say hi to us.

"Hey, guys. What are you up to?"

"Mom, can you leave us alone?" Pat says as soon as she has walked over to us.

"Stop, Pat, leave your mom alone. We like talking to her" Lily says.

"Okay then, well I will go then, since my son doesn't want me around. Do you guys want some lemonade or something?"

"No, Mom, can you just leave?" Pat says rather harshly.

"Actually, I would like some lemonade," Lily says.

"Yea, me too," says Thomas.

"What about you, Nicole and Jess, do you want some lemonade?"

"Yes, please," we both say.

"Okay. I'll be right back," she says looking over at Pat, smiling and then heading inside.

"Pat, you should be nice to your mom. At least she is normal, unlike my mom who is drunk all of the time," Thomas says.

Lily blurts out, "Yea, my mom is a freakin' lunatic. She is always drunk and yells at anyone who comes over. You should ask Thomas and Jess about the time they had to hide in my closet when they were over and my mom got home from work. She just yelled and screamed for like an hour and mopped up the floors and yelled about dirt."

"That was so scary," Thomas says, while laughing lightly, obviously remembering back to the day we were pressed against each other in Lily's closet.

"So the point is that you should be nice to your mom. You and Jess are like the only people I know that have normal parents," Lily adds.

I think about this for a moment, and am probably for the first time ever, truly grateful for my mother.

We drink lemonade, listen to some tunes, and it is soon time to leave. Although I had a fun day, I am actually happy to go home. I am more comfortable with my friends here than I would have been if it were just Pat and me, but I am definitely not one hundred percent myself. This is one of the major reasons that I was afraid to start dating one of my friends in the first place. I used to feel so comfortable around Pat, and now I feel so insecure and hyperaware of every move I make and every word I utter. I mean, I'm happy that we are finally going out, but I am ready to go home and be more in my element.

I hear my mom's tires pull into Pat's driveway, and then hear her horn give a quick beep.

We all start grabbing our stuff, and then Pat grabs my arm and pulls me over to the side of the yard, away from everyone else. He gives me a hug and says, "I'll call you later, okay?"

He then leans in to give me another kiss. I quickly give him a peck, even though I am pretty sure that it seems like he wanted to go in for a big kiss, but I am panicky because my mom is waiting, and I don't want her to see us.

"Bye, Pat," I say as I grab my backpack and head toward my mom's car where my friends are already sitting in the back seat and my mom is leaning out of the window talking to Pat's mom who is standing beside the driver's side window.

I quickly say, "Bye, Mrs. O'Malley. Thanks for the lemonade," before climbing into the passenger seat and closing my door. I turn around to look at my friends, and they are all just sitting there smiling at me and not saying anything. I quietly say, "Shut up," and turn back around, just as my mother is finally done talking to Mrs. O'Malley.

"Hey, guys, how was your day?" my mom asks us.

"Good," we say in unison.

I don't offer any more information. I lean into the radio, find something that isn't awful, and turn it up. My mom looks over at me, knowing that I don't want to talk about anything else right now. She puts her hand on my knee and gives it a little squeeze. Later, I will tell her that Pat and I are going out now. Right now, I just want to sit in the car and head home to my room and contentment.

Part 2

_____

AUGUST 1998

Chapter 14

A NEW WORLD

My world is falling apart. These pieces that were not understood for so many years have been put together. I wish I didn't know the truth. One day I felt like I understood everything. Now I am so confused. I am a jumble of emotions: I am angry, resentful, and dazed.

On Friday night, Nicole and Thomas woke me up at around midnight. I heard hysterical murmurings outside of my window followed by rushed taps on the glass. I heard Thomas loudly "shhhing" Nicole and her on the verge of tears. I opened the window, told them to be quiet, and that I would be out in a minute. As soon as I joined them in the street, I asked, "What's wrong?"

Nicole started crying hysterically and mumbling incomprehensible words through her tears. I just kept saying, "What?" I didn't understand any of what she was saying. So then Thomas explained everything, all while we continued to walk through the neighborhood, up and down the familiar streets that map out each of our childhoods.

He told me that an hour ago, he, Nicole, and Mr. Rosetti got back from Aunt Angela's house to find that Leanne was not home. Her car was gone from the driveway, which was weird considering the hour. They, at first, thought maybe she just went to 7-Eleven to get cigarettes. The strange thing was that the reason she didn't go with them to Aunt Angela's house in the first place was because she said that she was sick. So they started looking around the house for a note or something. Then they saw one of Leanne's vases thrown through the big screen TV in the living room. Nicole immediately yelled for her dad who was in the garage organizing some stuff. Mr. Rosetti said something like, "What the hell did she go and do now?" He then went into their bedroom to find drawers opened, clothes strewn about the room, and suitcases and travel bags laying all over the floor. In the bathroom there were broken perfume bottles, a broken red nail polish bottle, and makeup scattered all over the counter tops. I knew where this conversation was going before Thomas even finished his story. Leanne was gone. Her departure was something I could never have predicted, but was not entirely surprising either.

I had all of these thoughts going through my mind, none of which I could discern. Without really knowing what I was doing or saying, I dropped down to the street right below the giant pines and wept. Nicole and Thomas sat beside me in an Indian-style circle, and I leaned in and hugged my best friends. We all cried. Nicole screamed, and neither Thomas nor I told her to be quiet. We didn't care who woke up anymore. Leanne was gone and was not coming back.

Hours later, when I returned home, I had to wake my mother. I went right into her room, leaned over her, and shook her gently.

"Mom, wake up."

"Oh. It's you. You scared me. What's wrong?"

"Leanne ran away."

I knew it sounded childish and insignificant to what was actually going on, but that is all I could get out before I began crying and pouring out the whole story. She sat up in her bed, moved over, and patted the spot right next to her, indicating for me to climb in. I climbed under the covers, curled next to my mom, and immediately fell asleep.

I woke up to the smell of cooking. I opened my eyes. I was still in my mom's bed, but she was gone. I heard voices talking in the kitchen. I didn't understand what was going on until I remembered that it was my mom's weekend off from work. I quickly jumped out of bed and walked to the kitchen to see Nicole, Thomas, and my mom sitting at the kitchen table. If I didn't know any better, I would have said it was a beautiful scene. The kitchen smelled of home and happiness. The summer sun was sending a perfect beam of light directly to the center of the table, almost as if it was a spotlight focusing on a scene in a play. All of the people I loved most in the world were sitting around in the sun-soaked morning. However, I knew that the scene before me was a dismal one.

As soon as I saw Thomas and Nicole, I knew that they hadn't slept a wink. How they came to be here, eating raspberry pancakes with my mom, I had no idea.

"Come have some breakfast, Jess," my mom said as she placed a plate of steaming deliciousness in front of me. "Nicole and Thomas are going to stay with us for a while. I talked to Mr. Rosetti this morning."

Where this usually would have been an opportunity for rejoicing, none of us did more than nod our heads. In that moment, I knew that both my best friends' lives along with mine were somehow forever altered.

* * *

Thomas and Nicole ended up staying at my house for the last two weeks. They at first would sneak over in the middle of the night, until Mr. Rosetti just called my mom and asked if it was an inconvenience that two extra kids just appear every morning. When my mom told him that it was fine, he stopped calling.

The first few days my mom didn't mention anything about Leanne. By the third day, Thomas and Nicole seemed to be emerging from their fog a tiny bit and, in their diminishing shock, began to talk. They called Leann a heartless bitch. My mother, who usually would have at least asked that they not use that language, couldn't say a thing.

Lily stayed home during the nights, but would come over for breakfast every morning and stay until bedtime. She did spend a few nights, but our house had no extra rooms. And Thomas was already on the couch, and it was difficult for Lily, Nicole, and I to all fit on my single bed. We always made it work at Nicole's house, but often when it was all three of us, we would sleep in their basement or on the pullout couch, neither of which we had.

During the last few weeks, we spent our days in a haze. We talked about Leanne from time to time. We took turns crying—except for Thomas, of course; he just had liquid tears. We walked aimlessly. We went to the park and swung on the swings, but this time we didn't see who could kick our Converse the farthest. We smoked cigarettes underneath the pines in our smoking spot, but no one laughed. When I asked my mother how I could be there for them, she told me that sometimes just being present is all the support a friend needs. I guess Thomas and Nicole needed to spend every waking instant with the people they felt most comfortable with, just to make sure that we too wouldn't disappear.

Mr. Rosetti took one day off of work. After that, he went back to his normal routine of going to work, going to the gym, and getting home late. I felt angry with him for not being more upset. My mom explained to me that going about his routine was Mr. Rosetti's way of dealing with things. He couldn't sit around and cry; after all, it was Leanne's choice to go.

* * *

Today marks two weeks since Leanne left. It doesn't feel like things are getting better. Perhaps they are, but we have been going through the motions for so long now that we forgot what progress feels like. Every day feels the same. Nicole and I just woke up to the sound of Thomas and Lily's voices talking to my mother in the kitchen. I guess Lily already made it over here. It sounds like my mother is cooking us breakfast again. Is it the weekend already?

"Hey, Nicole, I'm going to go out and have some breakfast. You comin'?"

"No. I'm goin' to sleep a little longer."

"Okay, see you in a bit."

I climbed over Nicole, quietly shut the bedroom door, and walked into the kitchen.

"Hey, guys. Good morning."

"Hey, Jess."

"Hey, Ma, what are you cookin'?"

"Raspberry pancakes. Lily and Thomas were nice enough to go pick some in the yard while you slept the morning away."

"Slept the morning away. It can't be that late. What time is it?"

"It's nine thirty."

"That's not that late. Lily, what time did you get here?"

"I just got here a little while ago. Maybe like eight forty-five. I had my dad drop me off before he went to my grandma's."

"Oh, okay. What do you, guys, want to do today?"

I have asked my friends this same question every morning for the past two weeks not expecting a real answer. But I don't really know what else to talk about.

"Let's eat breakfast, and then go for a walk."

"Sounds good," both Thomas and I reply.

The pancakes are delicious. They taste like my mother and comfort and love and my best friends. I can't help but think about how unfair the world is. They taste so good, but all of a sudden, they get stuck in my throat. I think I'm going to cry. *Don't do it, Jess, don't do it!* I quickly grab my orange juice to drink down that lump of pancake sadness, and as soon as it slides down my throat, the tears start coming. It's not like a sobbing cry; it's more like a wet teary, red-faced weep. No one notices. Okay, now Lily notices.

"Hey, Jess, are you okay?" she asks.

"Yea. It's nothing" I reply.

"I was just thinking. It's nothing. It's over. I'm good now," I say as I wipe the tears from my face and force a small smile.

That is one way my friends are awesome. They know me so well. They know that I don't want to talk about it, so they leave it alone. Lily also knows exactly how to change the subject and not make it seem forced or awkward. She begins talking about her family and how they are going to their grandma's house today to visit her and how they wanted her to come, but how she didn't want to, and they got mad at her, etc. I only half hear what she is saying. I can't get the awful pictures out of my mind, but I know I need to keep trying. My mom told me how important it is to stay strong for my friends right now. I know that in order to create some sense of normalcy for them, I need to try not to get too emotional.

I make it through breakfast, and Nicole finally wakes up. We both quickly change out of our pajamas, and within minutes, the four of us are walking out of the house and down the street. Without anyone really saying, we walk straight past the pines and continue walking without any specific destination in mind. We eventually wind up at the edge of the woods that I, Thomas, and Nicole often played in as kids.

"Do you, guys, want to go in?" I ask.

"Yea. Let's see if that tree fort thingy is still there," Thomas says.

As kids, the three of us spent countless days in these woods, playing in a fort that seemed to be left just for us. I'm sure that some other generation of neighborhood kids made it, and then eventually stopped going as they got older, as we would eventually do too. But to us and our childhood, it was our Terabithia.

Thomas leads the way through the woods. When we get to where he thought the fort would be, we all stop and look around. We are all standing around looking in circles. Just when I'm about to declare that it must be gone, I see some red fabric peeking out between the leaves about twenty feet away.

"Hey, guys, look over there!" I excitedly exclaim, while pointing and already beginning my trek over there.

Not only is the fort still there, but it looks as if a new batch of neighborhood kids have taken it over and given it a complete make-over. There are curtains hung in the newly handcrafted windows. The main standing platform is painted a bright red, and each rung of the indisputably newly constructed ladder is painted a different vibrant color. There are all sorts of indicators that this fort is in constant use and is greatly loved. There are cushions, books, and even a pair of cheap kiddy binoculars strewn across the top. There are even some water bottles and some Goldfish cracker wrappers that seem to be anticipating their owners' return. I almost feel like an intruder in this

strangely magical and intimate kiddy world. It is so gratifying to realize that there are other kids who have found a haven in these woods
and in this fort, but I am also mournful of my lost innocence. I look
over at Thomas, and I know that he is feeling something similar to
what I am. We are all just staring at this beautiful picture of purity
when Thomas finally breaks the silence and says, "This is awesome."

There is a part of me, and I'm sure of everyone else that wants
to climb into this fort and be transported back to childhood for a
little while.

"I want to stay forever, but I feel like my badness is going to
seep through my veins and corrupt these poor innocent kids." This
escapes from Thomas's mouth with a chilling seriousness.

Normally this would be one of those things that we would all
start to laugh at him about because of how cheesy it sounds, but
not now. We all probably feel exactly the same way. Without saying
anything else, Thomas turns around and begins walking back out of
the woods toward the road. The rest of us follow without uttering a
word.

Chapter 15

GLIMMER

Today marks one month since the awfulness. It's like the first day I've felt like things may be getting better. I'm not sure exactly what made me come to this conclusion, but as I opened my eyes this morning, I felt the sun warming not only my pajama-laden body, but my tired soul. I know I haven't done much during this last month except exist, but existing without our usual dose of ridiculousness, laughter, and stretchy smiles has seemed to wear on me.

As I lay in bed with my Nicole on my left and my Lily on my right, I just sense that today is going to be better. My aunt and uncle and grandparents are coming over for a barbeque later today. My aunt and uncle I can do without, but I just love my grandparents to death.

I hear my mom banging around in the kitchen, and I want to get out there without waking up Lily or Nicole. I haven't had a moment alone with my mom for at least a month. I usually would take this as a welcome surprise, but she has been so understanding throughout everything that I feel kinda bad for the mean way I have treated her from time to time.

I am able to slowly creep out of bed without waking them. I turn the knob of my bedroom door and stealthily tiptoe up to my mom and hug her around the waist as she washes dishes.

"Uh. Oh my goodness, Jessica, you scared the living daylights out of me," my mother jumpily says as she turns around.

"Hi, Mama. I missed you."

"I haven't gone anywhere, Jessie girl. I've been right her."

"I know, Mom, but I haven't been able to really talk to you for like, weeks."

"I know, doll. But I know you've been busy being a good friend. That's what's most important right now."

"Yea, I know, Ma, I've just missed you."

"Well, I'm here now. It's just you and me. What do you want me to make you, guys, for breakfast today?"

"How about scrambled eggs and bacon?"

"You got it, girl." After a slight pause. "So what else is going on?"

"I don't know. Nothin' really I guess. I was just thinking about how weird it's going to be next year in school. You know. I always used to go over the Rosetti's in the morning before school, and Leanne was there. And when we would miss the bus in the morning, she would always drive us to school, because you were already at work. I know she wasn't always the best mom, but she had moments of greatness, you know. Do you remember when we were kids and you, guys, would always take us to the school's Easter egg hunt?"

"Of course."

"Yea, and like also whenever we would go camping, she would prepare for days making her famous macaroni salad and packing enough extra stuff not only for Nicole and Thomas, but also like extra stuff in case I ran out. And do you remember her amazing homemade pumpkin pies that she would make for Thanksgiving? I know that I am rambling, Mom, but she was good sometimes, you know?"

"I know, Jess."

My mother looked at me for a moment before she began again; she was probably selecting her words carefully.

"Jess, you need to realize that Leanne has been struggling with a lot of different things for a very long time. Even before Thomas and Nicole were born."

"I know, Mom."

"I love you and Matt very much."

Those words coming from her lips wrapped around me like one of those homemade wool blankets with all of the different-colored-stitched squares.

"I love you too, Mom."

My mom broke the momentary silence, "So, what do you, guys, think you are going to do today?"

"I don't know. Probably just hang out. If you want, maybe we can help you cook some of the food for the barbeque."

"That would be fun. Ask everyone when they wake up if they would even want to."

"Okay. Sounds good. I'm gonna go sit outside in the sun for a bit. If anyone wakes up, tell them I'm out there."

"Sounds good. Have fun."

As I step out the back door into the sweet, warm luxury of the summer morning's laziness, I prop myself on the warm back cement steps. I just marinate in the sun and begin to sweat almost immediately. However, it's not a bad sweat, but a cozy reminder of the time that I still have left with my beloved summer. I start thinking about Pat and how much he likes me. He calls me every night, but I don't stay on the phone with him longer than five minutes or so, because I'm always with my friends. I hate to admit it, but I love having them as an excuse to get off the phone. I mean, I really like having him as a boyfriend and love hanging out with him, but I hate how nothing is the same anymore. Now when we hang out, I feel like I can't quite act like myself. I find myself being too quiet. I hate the pressure to always have to kiss him and sit on his lap and hold his hand. I mean, I do like him, but I think I just want to be friends. How am I going to tell him? I just want things to go back to normal. I just want to hang out with my friends and roll around on the floor and burst out in song and say weird things and it be funny. I know I'm going to have to break up with him. I'm just so scared of messing things up for good. I guess if he can't understand how I feel, I shouldn't care either. This is definitely one of those things that is easier to say than it will be to act on.

"Hey, Jess," Lily says, forcing me back to reality.

"Hey, Lil."

"Whatcha doin' out here?"

"Just chillen'. Is anyone else up yet?"

"Nope."

"What are you thinkin' about?"

"Ughhhh. You don't even want to know."

"What?"

"I think I'm going to break up with Pat."

"Wow. Really? What's wrong?"

"I don't know. I just don't really want a boyfriend right now. I can't explain it."

"When do you think you are going to do it?"

"I don't know. Soon. Maybe later this afternoon."

"Wow. That's crazy. Well, if that's what you want to do."

"Yea. I think it is."

"Hey, guys," both Thomas and Nicole say as they march out the door and come join us on the stoop.

Thomas accidentally steps on my pinkie finger, and I automatically yell out, "Ow, you, bitch!"

This is the first time I have automatically responded with one of our old sayings. As soon as I say it, I realize that maybe I was too cheerful or maybe it's too soon to do that. I don't know where it came from; the words just launched themselves from my mouth. Luckily Thomas is not thinking of any of those things. He starts laughing, and the sound of his laughs wraps around me like a warm cozy scarf. I don't think anyone actually says anything, but we can't all fit on the stoop so we get up and move to the street directly in front of our house and sit in a circle.

"Hey, Jess, remember that time your mom got so mad at you because you told her she was old and boring, and she came over and started hitting you on the legs with her big plastic salad spoon. Then you started laughing because she made her crazy angry face. And it didn't hurt at all, and then the spoon broke, and she let out that long scream and was like, 'you broke my spoon!' and that made you laugh even harder," Thomas tells.

I reply, "Yes, I do. That was so freaking funny. Lily, do you remember the time that Thomas and I were hiding in your bedroom closet when your mom came home from work and she was running around the house screaming and scrubbing the floors, yelling that you messed up the house? Then Thomas banged his head on the wall in the closet, and your mom heard us and ran in the room as was like, 'What are you, assholes, doin' in there?' and we just ran right past her out of the house?"

Next Thomas relates, "Nicole, remember last year when you got suspended for coming back to school after lunch drunk, and you came home and put on your black cape and walked up and down the walkway on the side of our house in the pouring rain, saying that your life was over and that our dad was going to kill you?"

At the time, this was one of the most traumatic days of Nicole's life, but now, a year later, it is so funny to think of her all drunk, pacing in her black witch cape in the pouring rain. During that event, Nicole blamed me for getting in trouble, because I didn't talk her out of going to a classmate's house and drinking during the school day. I now realize how funny the whole thing is. We are all cracking up with that visual of Nicole taking over our heads.

As we continue to relay all of these funny and crazy memories of our years together, we are all laughing harder than we have in a while. Nicole was lying flat on her back at one point and couldn't stop laughing after Thomas told a story of them in their fat clothes stuffed with pillows. Nicole helped Thomas stuff so many pillows in his pants and shirt that he literally could not get up when Nicole pushed him down. He was laughing so hard trying to get up that he peed his pants. After the fat suit story, Lily laughed so hard that she got the hiccups, which made us laugh even more. I laughed so hard, my lungs hurt. As I sat there I realized that this is the first time that we have all laughed like this in a very long time; it feels amazing to have at least part of my friends back.

"Breakfast!" my mom yells out the back door.

We all get up and brush off the street pebbles from our thigh backs and walk into the house together.

Shortly after breakfast, we all gather in the kitchen to help my mom cook for the barbeque later. Lily and Thomas are in the dining room, peeling potatoes for my mom's famous German potato salad. Nicole is standing in the kitchen next to my mom, who is talking her through how to cut each vegetable that is placed before her. I am mixing the oil and vinegar and other ingredients for the salad dressing. I don't know why all of us cooking together is so fun, but it really is.

"Hey, Mom, I'll be right back. I'm going to put some music on."

I search through my CDs, but don't really find anything that all of us, including my mom would enjoy. So I go to Matt's room and knock on his door.

"Hey, Matt, it's me Jess."

"What?"

"Can I borrow a CD to listen to?"

"Sure, come in."

That is one nice thing about Matt; he really isn't weird about letting me borrow his stuff.

I look through his extensive CD collection, all classic rock, and decide that my mom would love to hear "America." I know that my mom and dad used to listen to them together, but she doesn't really associate with things like that as I think I would.

"Thanks, Matt. I'm going to put it on right now while we are cooking. I will bring it back as soon as I'm done."

I put the CD on and join my mom and Nicole back in the kitchen, while Thomas and Nicole continue to peel and cut potatoes. Cooking can be quite a monotonous task. The music plays on, and everyone is peeling and cutting and chopping and slicing. Not much talking is going on, but it seems that we all have found a rhythm. And it seems almost peaceful. I know my mom is happy with my music choice as she sings along to "A Horse with No Name." We maybe have only been in the kitchen for fifteen minutes when I hear a car door close out front.

"Hey, Ma…I think someone might be here already."

"It's, okay. All I really have left to put together is the potato salad. Can you go see who it is, Jess?"

"Yeah, sure."

I quickly wash my hands, and by the time I get to the front door, my grandparents are walking up the front walkway. I open the door and welcome them in with hugs and kisses.

"How are you, Jess?" my grandmother asks as she hands me an Entenmanns Ultimate Crumb Cake, my favorite.

"I'm good, Grandma."

I then give my grandpa a hug and kiss and ask him if he wants me to put on some tea water for him; he drinks tea even on the hottest summer days. He says yes, of course, and I go to turn on the water. I look at my mom, and she gives me a little eye roll. She gets annoyed that my grandpa always wants tea as soon as he walks in the door, especially in the dead of summer. My grandma sits at the table and begins talking to Lily and Thomas; it's not weird talking to them because she has known Thomas and Nicole forever and Lily for years. My grandpa sits on the couch and puts his feet up, waiting for his tea.

"Why don't you, kids, go outside and hang out now. Thank you so much for your help, but I can finish up here."

"Okay, Mom. C'mon, guys," I say as I grab the boom box and bring it outside.

I don't think my grandparents appreciated the music. I hate to turn it off when my mom seems to be enjoying it so much, but at least, I know she got some joy out of it.

Thomas, Lily, Nicole, and I head outside and sit under the table with the umbrella. I plug the music back in and continue where we left off with "America." We talk about nothing at first, just kind of sit around. Lily has brought out a can of the Nestea iced tea mix. She is eating it with a spoon. After taking a few spoonfuls, she passes it around the table.

Thomas breaks the silence. "How weird is school going to be next year?"

"What do you mean?" I ask.

"Well, you know, like my mom not being around for school shopping or in the morning when we are getting ready for school or after school to cook dinner."

"Yea, I guess so." I say.

I don't really know what else to say. I have been thinking the same thing for weeks.

We all sit in silence, passing the iced tea, thinking. I think only like a minute has passed, and my mom and grandparents come outside. Just as they are walking out, I see my aunt and uncle's car pull up out front.

I jump up and head to the street where their car is parked.

"Hey, Aunt Lynn. Hi, Uncle Jeff," I say as I hug each of them.

"What are you, kids, up to today?" she asks.

"Oh, nothin'. We're just hangin' out."

"Where's your mom?"

"She's inside with Grandma and Grandpa. You can go in."

"Hey, Lily, Thomas, and Nicole," she says as she passes by the table and heads inside.

"Hey, Aunt Lynn…Hey, Jeff," they say in unison.

As soon as they head inside, I am back at the table with my friends. Matt just came outside and sat at the table to join us.

If there was one thing that I had to come up with that described why I love my friends so much, it would have to be that feeling of comfort. When they are around my family and me, I don't have to feel shy or weird or wonder if anyone is going to say or do something to embarrass me. They are so ingrained in my life that I honestly can't remember what life was like before them.

We are all just sitting around getting ready to have a family barbecue. We are sitting in the backyard, listening to music, not really saying much, just existing. Today is nothing special really, but it crosses my mind that today is distinct. I summoned the idea up to the very edges of my consciousness very briefly earlier today, but now, I know for sure, we will all be okay.

About the Author

Jill Arland, a Long Island, New York, native, grew up frolicking along the beaches of the south shore. She received her Bachelor of Arts in Secondary Education with a concentration in English from SUNY New Paltz in Upstate New York. She then headed way down to Brooklyn where she received her Masters of Science in Special Education at Brooklyn College. Jill has now called the Denver, Colorado, area home for over a decade. Jill is currently a full-time secondary teacher but spends a majority of her free time with her head in a book or a pen in her hand. She enjoys doing very Colorado things like skiing, hiking, and camping with her husband, two kids, and a giant dog.

CPSIA information can be obtained
at www.ICGtesting.com
Printed in the USA
BVHW030828260321
603508BV00010B/35